TRAUMA

only one rule: no new text

SCHEMA 2.1

Schema 2.1

Schema 2.1 was published with:
2.2 Ivan Monroy Lopez · git2pod · Poetry
2.3 Audun Mortensen · Surf's Up (2010) · IMDB

J. R. Carpenter

Generation[s]

TRAUMAWIEN

first edition 2010

This book is only available at the online shop of Trauma Wien.
http://traumawien.at – verlag@traumawien.at

This book was set in Perpetua & Letter Gothic.
cover: Luc Gross & Julian Palacz
production: Julian Palacz
edit: Luc Gross

Table of Contents

FIRST GENERATION

Excerpts from the Chronicles of Pookie & JR

Excerpts from the Chronicles of Pookie & JR:
Previously, Pookie and JR had only ever met at parties.
For the first few nights, Pookie and JR keep to their corners.
Pookie hides in his cup when JR is in her cups.
The next morning, JR goes for a long walk; Pookie does not.
Pookie only plays in his water dish when he has an audience.
Pookie slowly comes out of his shell, so to speak.
Pookie has many shells to choose from.
Do you hear that? JR asks Pookie.
To be continued...

Excerpts from the Chronicles of Pookie & JR:
Garbage collection is Monday and Thursday.
Tuesday mornings, a cleaning woman comes.
Pookie has many shells to choose from.
The contents of JR's suitcase spill across the polished floor.
Sometimes JR adds a strawberry or a raisin to Pookie's feeding dish.
Pookie keeps his thoughts to himself.
JR is in between homes.
To be continued…

Excerpts from the Chronicles of Pookie & JR:
Previously, Pookie and JR had only ever met at parties.
Pookie is actually pretty social, for a hermit crab.
Garbage collection is Monday and Thursday.
Tuesday mornings, a cleaning woman comes.
Pookie has many shells to choose from.
The contents of JR's suitcase spill across the polished floor.
Tonight's dinner puts one withered leek out of its misery.
Do you hear that? JR asks Pookie.
JR hasn't been sleeping much lately.
To be continued...

J.R. Carpenter Packing to move is so unpleasant I'm considering never unpacking. What do you say, suitcases? Shall we run off together & live at the Ritz?
14 June 2009 at 14:55 · Comment · Like

Allan Lento I stayed at the ritz and it's not that expensive!
14 June 2009 at 15:20 · Delete

Lissa Holloway-Attaway meet you there!
14 June 2009 at 15:31 · Delete

Erin Moure not even suitcases... take Air Canada to Zurich and when you get there, they will have lost your bags for days: utter freedom and the gift of the possible!
14 June 2009 at 15:48 · Delete

John Worthington That's why I don't plan to move again.
14 June 2009 at 16:19 · Delete

J.R. Carpenter Erin - that's a brilliant plan!
14 June 2009 at 16:24 · Delete

Michael Boyce unfortunately or not never unpacking is like very much like always still packing, and losing your bags can mean that you always can wonder where they are and what was in them anyway, which again is like packing always - is packing to move like packing to stay - and what is packing anyway? and what is gift wrapping and how is that like packing or not?
14 June 2009 at 17:07 · Delete

Write a comment...

Excerpts from the Chronicles of Pookie & JR:
JR is patient; Pookie has to crawl before he can walk.
Pookie is actually pretty social, for a hermit crab.
Tuesday mornings, a cleaning woman comes.
JR hasn't been sleeping much lately.
Pookie keeps his thoughts to himself.
To be continued…

Excerpts from the Chronicles of Pookie & JR:
For the first few nights, Pookie and JR keep to their corners.
Pookie watches, but what does he see?
JR apologizes to Pookie for talking on the phone for so long.
Every three days or so, JR waters the ferns.
Pookie and JR exchange knowing glances.
Hermit crabs make excellent roommates, JR thinks.
JR crumbles Pookie's hermit crab food pellets into bite-sized bits.
JR hasn't been sleeping much lately.
JR is in between homes.
To be continued...

J.R. Carpenter Have just discovered - to my delight- that Skype was invented by a guy named Janus. The double-headed god of peer-to-peer.
23 June 2009 at 00:12 · Comment · Like

Gordon Bradley and Gregory Chatonsky like this.

Write a comment...

J.R. Carpenter Limbering up before my daily length in the tub.
22 June 2009 at 16:51 · Comment · Like

Kate Pullinger likes this.

Write a comment...

J.R. Carpenter In the window covering department, ferns are much preferable to curtains.
21 June 2009 at 15:00 · Comment · Like

Penn Kemp likes this.

Write a comment...

J.R. Carpenter Hermit crabs make excellent roommates.
20 June 2009 at 17:50 · Comment · Like

At 05:00 AM 22/06/2009, Ingrid Bachmann wrote:

Hi J.R.

Glad to hear that you are enjoying the peace and quiet.
Thanks so much for taking care of Pookie, plants and mail.

Best

Ingrid

Excerpts from the Chronicles of Pookie & JR:
The next morning, JR goes for a long walk; Pookie does not.
Pookie is actually pretty social, for a hermit crab.
Pookie and JR exchange knowing glances.
Live and let live, Pookie's nonchalant attitude seems to suggest.
Hermit crabs make excellent roommates, JR thinks.
Pookie has turned JR off of shellfish for life.
Tonight's dinner puts one withered leek out of its misery.
Late one night, Pookie and JR listen to a chained dog's howls.
To be continued...

Excerpts from the Chronicles of Pookie & JR:
JR has a friend over for drinks and forgets to introduce Pookie.
Tuesday mornings, a cleaning woman comes.
The contents of JR's suitcase spill across the polished floor.
The cafe across the street is only noisy until eleven or so.
Do you hear that? JR asks Pookie.
Pookie keeps his thoughts to himself.
To be continued…

Excerpts from the Chronicles of Pookie & JR:
Previously, Pookie and JR had only ever met at parties.
JR has a friend over for drinks and forgets to introduce Pookie.
JR is patient; Pookie has to crawl before he can walk.
Pookie only plays in his water dish when he has an audience.
Pookie is actually pretty social, for a hermit crab.
Pookie has many shells to choose from.
The contents of JR's suitcase spill across the polished floor.
JR is in between homes.
JR is in hiding.
To be continued…

LAPSUS LINGUAE, June 24, 2009

Excerpts from the Chronicles of Pookie& JR

Last week I was hanging out with Nick Montfort in Montreal. He's been working on a series of 1k story generators written in Python. I've never paid any attention to Python before, because it doesn't output to the web. To download and run Nick's 1k story generators in a terminal window, visit: http://grandtextauto.org/2008/11/30/three-1k-story-generators/

This week I'm hanging out with Ingrid Bachmann's hermit crab Pookie. Pookie is a biological, digital, quasi-fictional manifestation of Ingrid Bachmann's imagination. Pookie already has a website: http://www.digitalhermit.ca. And I've already written about past collaborations between Bachmann and Pookie: Digital Crustaceans v.0.2: Homesteading on the Web: http://luckysoap.com/stories/bachmann_and_pookie.html. But I've never spent any time alone with a hermit crab before. I started chronicling my adventures with Pookie as sentences written on a blackboard, and then started feeding those sentences into one of Nick's story generators written Python. The generator uses a sequence of (specially written) sentences; all but 5-9 sentences are removed and the remaining text is presented as the story.

http://luckysoap.com/lapsuslinguae/2009/06/excerpts-from-the-chronicles-of-pookie-jr/

Excerpts from the Chronicles of Pookie & JR:
So far, Pookie has refused to be engaged in conversation.
Pookie watches, but what does he see?
Pookie has many shells to choose from.
JR has been wearing the same shirt for days now.
When Pookie digs in the night, he makes quite a racket.
To be continued…

J.R. Carpenter

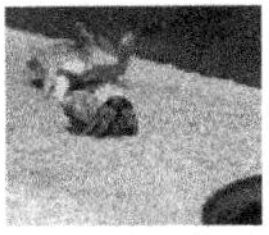

Excerpts from the Chronicles of Pookie & JR

Last week I was hanging out with Nick Montfort in Montreal. He's been working on a series of 1k story generators written in Python. I've never paid any attention to Python before, because it doesn't output to the web...

24 June 2009 at 16:11 · Comment · Like · Share

RECENT ACTIVITY

J.R. attended St.Jean sur St.Viateur. · Comment · Like

J.R. likes Rob McLennan's note 12 or 20 questions: second series.

J.R. and Isabelle Lelarge are now friends. · Comment · Like

J.R. Carpenter Merrily ripping off / riffing on Nick Montfort's 1k Python story generators http://preview.tinyurl.com/696wqw
23 June 2009 at 16:47 · Comment · Like

Rita Raley, Talan Memmott and Scott Rettberg like this.

Scott Rettberg We should do a special issue of a journal composed of nothing but hacks of Nick's programs.
23 June 2009 at 16:54 · Delete

J.R. Carpenter totally!
23 June 2009 at 19:27 · Delete

Write a comment...

At 10:23 AM 25/06/2009, Ingrid Bachmann wrote:

Hi J.R.,

What a lovely message on Facebook. I am glad that Pookie is providing stimulation. I am glad you are there. Your intellect will stimulate him as well. What a good writer you are – I always think that anew after reading your work – no surprise really, but it is such a pleasant surprise.

Take care and thanks again for looking after things.

All the best,

Ingrid

Excerpts from the Chronicles of Pookie & JR:
Tuesday mornings, a cleaning woman comes.
Pookie has many shells to choose from.
Hermit crabs make excellent roommates, JR thinks.
Pookie has turned JR off of shellfish for life.
When Pookie digs in the night, he makes quite a racket.
To be continued…

Excerpts from the Chronicles of Pookie & JR:
JR has a friend over for drinks and forgets to introduce Pookie.
JR apologizes to Pookie for talking on the phone for so long.
Pookie and JR exchange knowing glances.
The contents of JR's suitcase spill across the polished floor.
JR crumbles Pookie's hermit crab food pellets into bite-sized bits.
Pookie's full name is Pookie 14.
To be continued…

Excerpts from the Chronicles of Pookie & JR:
Previously, Pookie and JR had only ever met at parties.
For the first few nights, Pookie and JR keep to their corners.
The next morning, JR goes for a long walk; Pookie does not.
Pookie only plays in his water dish when he has an audience.
Pookie is actually pretty social, for a hermit crab.
JR changes Pookie's water. Pookie makes a mess of his feeding dish.
To be continued…

Excerpts from the Chronicles of Pookie & JR:
The next morning, JR goes for a long walk; Pookie does not.
Sometimes JR adds a strawberry or a raisin to Pookie's feeding dish.
Late one night, Pookie and JR listen to a chained dog's howls.
Pookie's full name is Pookie 14.
JR is in hiding.
To be continued...

J.R. Carpenter Nick Montfort blogs my Pookie & JR remix of his Python story generator: http://bit.ly/YpDCN
11 July 2009 at 15:52 · Comment · Like

J.R. Carpenter If I keep waking up this early I will have to move to Europe, where, by now, it is a reasonable time of day and everyone's had a coffee.
10 July 2009 at 11:50 · Comment · Like

Pascal-Denis Lussier But if you moved to Australia it would be tonight, and you could sleep in!
10 July 2009 at 12:16 · Delete

Scott Rettberg Not a bad idea.
10 July 2009 at 13:00 · Delete

Write a comment...

J.R. Carpenter Good morning all you fictional characters. Now, where were we?
09 July 2009 at 15:57 · Comment · Like

"J. R. Carpenter, author of *Words the Dog Knows, Entre Ville, The Cape,* and other fine works of e-lit, print, and xerography, has delightfully re-purposed one of my 1k story generators to have it tell stories involving her and a hermit crab named Pookie. The program has grown to about 2k, but it uses the same simple (and surprisingly effective) method as my first generator does: It simply removes all but 5-9 sentences from a sequence, eliding some of what's been written. Sometimes the reader is left to wonder who the hermit is."

Nick Montfort, Post Position: http://nickm.com/post/2009/07/story-generation-with-pookie-and-jr/

Excerpts from the Chronicles of Pookie & JR:
For the first few nights, Pookie and JR keep to their corners.
JR has a friend over for drinks and forgets to introduce Pookie.
Pookie watches, but what does he see?
Pookie only plays in his water dish when he has an audience.
Tuesday mornings, a cleaning woman comes.
JR has been wearing the same shirt for days now.
The contents of JR's suitcase spill across the polished floor.
JR crumbles Pookie's hermit crab food pellets into bite-sized bits.
To be continued...

Excerpts from the Chronicles of Pookie & JR:
JR has a friend over for drinks and forgets to introduce Pookie.
Pookie slowly comes out of his shell, so to speak.
Pookie is actually pretty social, for a hermit crab.
Pookie and JR exchange knowing glances.
Hermit crabs make excellent roommates, JR thinks.
Sometimes JR adds a strawberry or a raisin to Pookie's feeding dish.
JR cooks slowly, foraging in this strange kitchen.
Tonight's dinner puts one withered leek out of its misery.
To be continued...

Excerpts from the Chronicles of Pookie & JR:
So far, Pookie has refused to be engaged in conversation.
Tuesday mornings, a cleaning woman comes.
The contents of JR's suitcase spill across the polished floor.
When Pookie digs in the night, he makes quite a racket.
JR hasn't been sleeping much lately.
To be continued…

Excerpts from the Chronicles of Pookie & JR:
Previously, Pookie and JR had only ever met at parties.
Pookie has many shells to choose from.
Live and let live, Pookie's nonchalant attitude seems to suggest.
The cafe across the street is only noisy until eleven or so.
JR hasn't been sleeping much lately.
Pookie's full name is Pookie 14.
To be continued…

Excerpts from the Chronicles of Pookie & JR:
For the first few nights, Pookie and JR keep to their corners.
Every three days or so, JR waters the ferns.
Hermit crabs make excellent roommates, JR thinks.
Pookie has turned JR off of shellfish for life.
Pookie's full name is Pookie 14.
JR is in hiding.
To be continued...

At 08:21 AM 06/07/2009, Ingrid Bachmann wrote:

Hey JR,

Thanks for taking such good care of Pookie and the place, it looks great. Thanks also for the lovely blackboard diary. Perhaps we can touch base tomorrow or Tuesday morning? I'm heading out for Halifax Tuesday afternoon.

Look forward to talking to you.

Best,

Ingrid

SOURCE CODE: PookieAndJR.py

```
#Story generation by Nick Montfort
#Story by J.R. Carpenter
#2009-06-24
#Thanks to Ingrid & Pookie
from random import choice
while True:
 s=['Previously, Pookie and JR had only ever met at parties',
    'For the first few nights, Pookie and JR keep to their corners',
    'So far, Pookie has refused to be engaged in conversation',
    'JR has a friend over for drinks and forgets to introduce Pookie',
    'Pookie hides in his cup when JR is in her cups',
    'Pookie watches, but what does he see?',
    'The next morning, JR goes for a long walk; Pookie does not',
    'JR is patient; Pookie has to crawl before he can walk',
    'Pookie only plays in his water dish when he has an audience',
    'JR apologizes to Pookie for talking on the phone for so long',
    'Pookie slowly comes out of his shell, so to speak',
    'Pookie is actually pretty social, for a hermit crab',
    'Every three days or so, JR waters the ferns',
    'Garbage collection is Monday and Thursday',
    'Tuesday mornings, a cleaning woman comes',
    'Pookie and JR exchange knowing glances',
    'Pookie has many shells to choose from',
    'JR has been wearing the same shirt for days now',
    'The contents of JR\'s suitcase spill across the polished floor',
    'Live and let live, Pookie\'s nonchalant attitude seems to suggest',
    'Hermit crabs make excellent roommates, JR thinks',
    'JR changes Pookie\'s water. Pookie makes a mess of his feeding dish',
    'JR crumbles Pookie\'s hermit crab food pellets into bite-sized bits',
    'Sometimes JR adds a strawberry or a raisin to Pookie\'s feeding dish',
    'Pookie will eat miniscule amounts of anything except meat and dairy',
    'Pookie has turned JR off of shellfish for life',
    'JR cooks slowly, foraging in this strange kitchen',
    'Tonight\'s dinner puts one withered leek out of its misery',
    'The cafe across the street is only noisy until eleven or so',
    'When Pookie digs in the night, he makes quite a racket',
    'Late one night, Pookie and JR listen to a chained dog\'s howls',
    'Do you hear that? JR asks Pookie',
    'JR hasn\'t been sleeping much lately',
    'Pookie keeps his thoughts to himself',
    'Pookie\'s full name is Pookie 14',
    'JR is in between homes',
```

```
  'JR is in hiding']
l=choice(range(5,10))
while len(s)>l:
 s.remove(choice(s))
print "\nExcerpts from the Chronicles of Pookie & JR:\n"+'.\n'.join(s)+'.'
raw_input('To be continued...')
```

DOWNLOAD: http://luckysoap.com/generation/PookieAndJR.zip

Download the python file to your desktop and unzip. On a Mac or Linux system, you can run the story generator by opening a Terminal Window, typing "cd Desktop", and typing "python PookieAndJR.py". Hint: look for Terminal in your Utilities folder. These Python story generator runs on Windows, too, but you will probably need to install Python first: http://www.python.org/download/releases/2.6.5/. Once Python is installed, double click on the file and it will automatically launch and run in a terminal window. Every time you press ENTER a new version of the story will appear.

The Rajakumar Iteration

In July 2009, NYC-based artist/programmer Ravi Rajakumar ported the Python script into Javascript to create this web browser friendly version of the Chronicles of Pookie & JR: http://luckysoap.com/pookieandjr/index.html

J.R. Carpenter

The Saga of Pookie & JR Continues

Back in June I adapted Nick Montfort's 1k Python story generator to document my adventures with Ingrid Bachmann's hermit crab Pookie in The Chronicles of Pookie & JR: http://luckysoap.com/lapsuslinguae/2009/06/excerpts-from-chronicles-of-pookie-jr.htmlNick went on to post about it on his blog, Post...

16 July 2009 at 01:36 · Comment · Like · Share

Christine Wilks likes this.

Ravi Rajakumar Cool to see it up! By the way, the date stamp on your version of it, JR, is June 24th, which was my birthday.
16 July 2009 at 04:26 · Delete

Michael Boyce this is fantastic - lots to be said about this - someone should, someone will i'm sure, but i'll just say it's great - and ravi, a lot of stuff sure happened on your birthday, eh?
19 July 2009 at 20:29 · Delete

Write a comment...

SOURCE CODE: http://luckysoap.com/pookieandjr/index.html

```
<html xmlns="http://www.w3.org/1999/xhtml">
<head>
<meta http-equiv="Content-Type" content="text/html; charset=UTF-8" />
<title>Pookie and JR</title>
<link href="reset.css" rel="stylesheet" type="text/css" />
<link href="pnjr.css" rel="stylesheet" type="text/css" />
<script xmlns="" type="text/javascript" src="http://code.jquery.com/
jquery-latest.js"></script>
<script xmlns="" type="text/javascript" src="http://jqueryui.com/latest/
ui/ui.core.js"></script>
<script xmlns="" type="text/javascript" src="http://ajax.googleapis.com/
ajax/libs/jqueryui/1.7.2/jquery-ui.min.js"></script>
<script type="text/javascript" src="pnjr.js"></script>
</head>

 <body>
 <div id="mainframe">
  <div id="storyframe"></div>
  <a href="#" onclick="writeStory();return false;">To be continued...
  </a>
  </div>
</body>
</html>
```

SOURCE CODE: http://luckysoap.com/pookieandjr/pnjr.js

```
/* Story generation by Nick Montfort
  Story by J.R. Carpenter
  2009-06-24
  Thanks to Ingrid & Pookie
  Ported to Javascript by Ravi Rajakumar
  2009-07-15 */

$(document).ready(function(){writeStory();});


function writeStory() {
         $("#storyframe").html(buildStory());
}

function buildStory() {
var story = "<h1>Excerpts from the Chronicles of Pookie & JR:</h1>";
story = story + makeStoryArray().join('.<br/>') + '.';
return story;
}

function makeStoryArray() {
var s=['Previously, Pookie and JR had only ever met at parties',
   'For the first few nights, Pookie and JR keep to their corners',
   'So far, Pookie has refused to be engaged in conversation',
   'JR has a friend over for drinks and forgets to introduce Pookie',
   'Pookie hides in his cup when JR is in her cups',
   'Pookie watches, but what does he see?',
   'The next morning, JR goes for a long walk; Pookie does not',
   'JR is patient; Pookie has to crawl before he can walk',
   'Pookie only plays in his water dish when he has an audience',
   'JR apologizes to Pookie for talking on the phone for so long',
   'Pookie slowly comes out of his shell, so to speak',
   'Pookie is actually pretty social, for a hermit crab',
   'Every three days or so, JR waters the ferns',
   'Garbage collection is Monday and Thursday',
   'Tuesday mornings, a cleaning woman comes',
   'Pookie and JR exchange knowing glances',
   'Pookie has many shells to choose from',
   'JR has been wearing the same shirt for days now',
   'The contents of JR\'s suitcase spill across the polished floor',
   'Live and let live, Pookie\'s nonchalant attitude seems to suggest',
   'Hermit crabs make excellent roommates, JR thinks',
   'JR changes Pookie\'s water. Pookie makes a mess of his feeding dish',
```

```
   'JR crumbles Pookie\'s hermit crab food pellets into bite-sized bits',
   'Sometimes JR adds a strawberry or a raisin to Pookie\'s feeding dish',
   'Pookie will eat miniscule amounts of anything except meat and dairy',
   'Pookie has turned JR off of shellfish for life',
   'JR cooks slowly, foraging in this strange kitchen',
   'Tonight\'s dinner puts one withered leek out of its misery',
   'The cafe across the street is only noisy until eleven or so',
   'When Pookie digs in the night, he makes quite a racket',
   'Late one night, Pookie and JR listen to a chained dog\'s howls',
   'Do you hear that? JR asks Pookie',
   'JR hasn\'t been sleeping much lately',
   'Pookie keeps his thoughts to himself',
   'Pookie\'s full name is Pookie 14',
   'JR is in between homes',
   'JR is in hiding'];

var choice = Math.ceil(Math.random()*5)+5;
var whichCut = 0;
while (s.length > choice) {
         whichCut = Math.ceil(Math.random()*s.length)-1;
         s.splice(whichCut,1);
         }
return s;
}
```

Ingrid Bachmann: Digital Crustaceans v.0.2: Homesteading on the Web

Ingrid Bachmann can't sit still. Toiling for hours at keyboard and monitor is not her idea of a good time. Throughout her long-standing interest in Internet technology she has sought ways to bridge the physical / digital divide. To this end Bachmann has enlisted the aid of collaborator, Pookie the Hermit Crab. In v.0.1 of The Digital Crustaceans project, Pookie – a biological, digital, quasi-fictional manifestation – explores a fascinating corner of the web at http://www.digitalhermit.ca/, a site first created for "Science Fair," curated and organized by Lorraine Oades at StudioXX, Montréal, Québec (2002).[1]

In the installation iteration, "Digital Crustaceans v.0.2: Homesteading on the Web," presented at Gallery Articule, Main Gallery, April 4 – May 4 2003, Bachmann breaks the shackles of the monitor, employing multiple modes of representation to draw a relationship between the nomadic nature of the hermit crab and the cultural exercise of navigating on the web. Bachmann states: "This project views the Web as more than an address in cyberspace for the exchange of information of promotion; it views the Web as a form of organic architecture to be worked in and on and across."

1 On http://www.digitalhermit.ca/ Ingrid Bachmann writes:
Hermit crabs are families of crustaceans that make their homes and shelters in the unused or abandoned gastropod shells of snails and mollusks. Unlike other crustaceans, to whom they are related, hermit crabs do not carry their houses with them. They live in the discarded shells of other crustaceans, when they outgrow a shell they abandon it and find another.
In this project, I wanted to be a hermit crab on the World Wide Web, to work in existing sites and spaces. This was not conceived as a pirate or graffiti project as such, I wanted to occupy spaces and work within existing frameworks that allowed for occupation and modification. After working on the project, I realized the site of this project was not individual web sites but the system of information dissemination itself – the routing of information through international server routes and the actual physical routes of the internet – the fibre optic cables, submarine cables and communication cables that constitute the material base of the Internet.
The home site or page of this project is a terrarium, located in Montreal, the home of a real hermit crab, Pookie*, whose explorations of his own habitat become the basis for the viewer's explorations in cyberspaces.

*Pookie is an arbitrary unit of measurement used in cyberspace

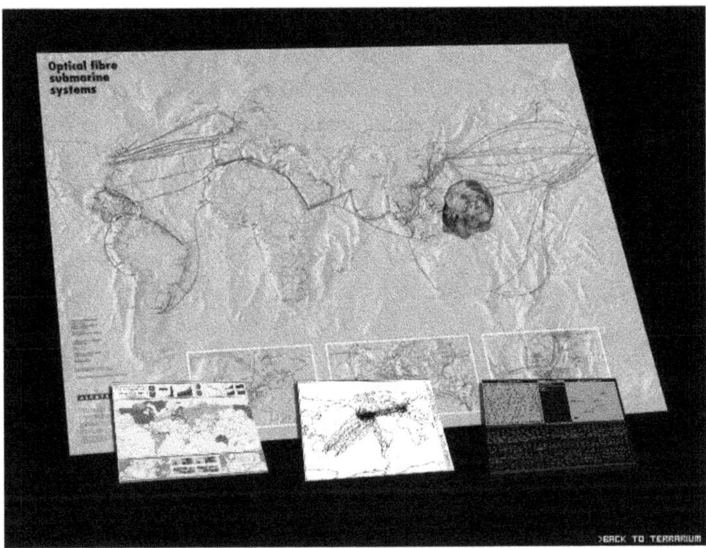

Screenshot from http://www.digitalhermit.ca/

We usually think of a hermit as one who stays at home. Since the hermit crab carries its home on its back, home may be anywhere – why not on the internet? Indeed, Pookie leads a double life. Ensconced in a swank steel and glass tank, the real live Pookie's every move is charted by a ceiling mounted motion detector. Bachmann collaborated with ArtEngine, an Ottawa based technology art collective; programmers Alexandre Castonguay and Mathieu Bouchard wrote the custom software that translates the motion capture of Pookie's wanderings to an ancient-sounding Hp 7475A Plotter. The record of this digital hermit's adventures, printed out over the course of the day, indicate that he does not travel far. He moves slowly, not having evolved much these past millions of years. Nonetheless, as a biological entity he directs technological impulses as deftly as a hand on a mouse; with the smallest organic movements, Pookie sets a global infrastructure into motion along the way.

In two large drawings on the gallery wall, the once mythic architecture of cyberspace is represented in a most tangible form: five feet tall and painted in orange and lime green, "Router level Interconnectivity of the

Internet" looks like a giant, blood-shot eyeball. Larger still, a map of the world in heavy, painted lines: "Optical Fibre Submarine Systems Across the Globe," represents the subterranean cables which constitute part of the Internet's material base in rough, coloured string. The antiquated backbone of the internet depicted evokes the fragility of infrastructure; a weakness we are kept blissfully unaware of in the high speed, eye-candy strip mall that is now the internet's public face. The instability of the internet remains a point of hope for Bachmann: only because it is such a porous and unstable medium will the internet continue to provide an alternative site for different points of view, continued easy access, and hacker and shareware freedoms.

Drawing on her long history of drawing, Bachmann presents a series of watercolours with fanciful titles depicting the life and times of Pookie. An archetypal figure for the twenty-first century, Pookie is the real star of the show. The titles of the drawings form a narrative of concern: "Pookie has an existential moment," "Pookie worries about the world," and "Pookie ponders the great religions of the world and finds them wanting." The state of the web is a vast subject; our task as humans is a difficult one – to grasp, ensure and maintain our place in this global technology. A wild depiction of "the hermit crab's cosmology" reminds us: all systems are precarious. In "Pookie in an unnatural habitat," Pookie the web crawler appears most uncomfortable lodged in a painting of vivid flowers. Perhaps, we are all becoming more at ease homesteading anonymously on the web. On the Internet no one knows you're a hermit crab.

Bachmann's exploration of the "earthly realities of digital technologies" also includes a hilarious series of Photoshoped images of Pookie in outer space. In one image the intrepid Pookie, just visible through the glass visor of a space suit's helmet, is "The first hermit crab on the moon." In a collection of snapshots, "Pookie explores the telecommunication satellites that constitute the wireless network infrastructures of the internet". Through Pookie, Bachmann performs "the sleight-of-hand replacement of the concrete, objective world of life as it is lived with the subtle and ephemeral world of fiction"[2] with a quixotic humour and charm rare to the internet these days.

The arcane and mysterious language of biology used in Bachmann's water-colour titles define the common hermit crab: Phylum: Arthopoda; Sub-Phylum: Crustacea; Order: Decapdoa; and so on. These distinguishing characteristics contrast nicely with the oblique language of Internet Technology we are so readily versant in today. The minutia / human interest story of Pookie the natural history specimen or Pookie the space-crab may or may not be more real to us, more easily grasped than the still murky backbone of the internet. Does the average human know what a router is or are they more likely to know what hermit crabs eat?

Bachmann first became involved with the internet at the Banff Centre in the early 90's. She went there as an artist in residence and stayed for two years as a facilitator in the artist in residency program. "There was a lot of interest in technology, internet, vr, everything. There was also an incredible spirit of openness and experimentation". Bachmann's earlier Internet related projects include, "Nomad Web: Sleeping Beauty Awakes," an network project exploring women's relationship to technology at the Walter Phillips Gallery in Banff, Alberta (1993-1994); and "Fault Lines/ Lignes de Faille: Measurement, Distance and Place, Mesure, distance et lieu," in collaboration with Barbara Layne, at La Centrale, Montréal, Québec and Side Street Projects, Santa Monica, California (1995).

As the version release numbers indicate, Digital Crustaceans v.0.2 is by no means finished. A forward-looking project, it ponders big questions: if the web is democracy – what kind of democracy will it become? It poses digital questions in biological terms. As the motion detector and I stare the slow-moving, unflappable Pookie down, I think about how quick humans are to evolve. Whether it's good for us or not we tend to run wildly off into all aspects of readily accessible, but at times, barely assessable culture. The principles of homesteading are slower, more deliberate. The hermit crab is our emissary as he ventures out gamely – an innocent, a scavenger, a real-estate guru on the wild frontier of the web.

2 Mario Vargas Llosa, Letters to a Young Novelist, New York: Picador, 1997. page 7.

SECOND GENERATION

I've Died and Gone to Devon

I've died and gone to Devon.
England is a small country, unless you're driving across it.
From the M3/A303 you'd think the whole country was countryside.
A full moon whitewashes the hoot-owl-haunted high-tide river.
Cumulus sheep graze the high hill across from the house.
Dartmouth, Devon, is 98% prettier than Dartmouth, Nova Scotia.
BBQs in Devon are just like BBQs in Nova Scotia: eventually it rains.
On rainy days someone always says: A little rain never hurt anyone.
The fields get so muddy it's no wonder the cows around here are brown.
A pair of swans swans about near the slipway at Blackness.
This is an achingly beautiful place to come across a little death.

I've died and gone to Devon.
England is a small country, unless you're driving across it.
If this is the wrong side of the road, I don't care what's right.
A full moon whitewashes the hoot-owl-haunted high-tide river.
We brave the rain to raid the orchard. Wet plums fall into waiting hands.
The sea floats above a wave of hills, a thin strip bluer than the sky.
The Dart runs from Dartmoor, south to open its muddy mouth to the sea.
BBQs in Devon are just like BBQs in Nova Scotia: eventually it rains.
The sky clears. High cloud shadows race across field-carved crooked hills.
A half moon rises over Dittisham. We row down for a half at Ferry Boat Inn.
This is an achingly beautiful place to come across a little death.

I've died and gone to Devon.
England is a small country, unless you're driving across it.
From the M3/A303 you'd think the whole country was countryside.
If this is the wrong side of the road, I don't care what's right.
Meanders, bends in the river, don't last forever, but this house might.
A full moon whitewashes the hoot-owl-haunted high-tide river.
I lie awake thinking about the Dart carving its path through the night.
It's solid black night until late moonlight proves the vast water.
Cormorants line the riverbank, great wings hanging like laundry to dry.
This is an achingly beautiful place to come across a little death.

J.R. Carpenter I've died and gone to Devon.
19 August 2009 at 15:29 · Comment · Like

Christine Wilks, Nora Maynard and Carolyn Guertin like this.

Kenny Doren Do tell.
19 August 2009 at 15:40 · Delete

Elisabeth Belliveau yup , totally need more details . . .
19 August 2009 at 17:47 · Delete

J.R. Carpenter this place is so insanely beautiful my heart stopped at least eight times during the car ride here (ok, that may have been due to driving wrong side on winding country lanes high-walled by greenery and too narrow for two cars to pass). i will post pictures soon, but they won't do justice to this heaven in Devon i've landed in.
19 August 2009 at 18:49 · Delete

Cris Cheek are u sure you were on the wrong side of the road ?
20 August 2009 at 04:54 · Delete

Write a comment...

I've died and gone to Devon.
The three-hour drive from Heathrow to the West Country really takes four.
How does rain on magnolia leaves produce a dry, rustling sound?
On a clear day, from the top of the drive we can see south to the sea.
From the lower drive, a view of the Dart opens north to Totnes.
The fields get so muddy it's no wonder all the cows around here are brown.
This is an achingly beautiful place to come across a little death.

I've died and gone to Devon.
A full moon whitewashes the hoot-owl-haunted high-tide river.
How does rain on magnolia leaves produce a dry, rustling sound?
Cumulus sheep graze the high hill across from the house.
It's an hour's walk to Totnes, along the Dart Valley footpath.
I lie awake thinking about the Dart carving its path through the night.
Fish & Chips taste best by the seaside. Same goes for crab sandwiches.
This is an achingly beautiful place to come across a little death.

I've died and gone to Devon.
In North America, roads this narrow wouldn't even count as driveways.
We brave the rain to raid the orchard. Wet plums fall into waiting hands.
Fish & Chips taste best by the seaside. Same goes for crab sandwiches.
The very idea of the sea is hard to believe in, in rain and fog and dark.
A half moon rises over Dittisham. We row down for a half at Ferry Boat Inn.
This is an achingly beautiful place to come across a little death.

I've died and gone to Devon.
The three-hour drive from Heathrow to the West Country really takes four.
If this is the wrong side of the road, I don't care what's right.
Sharpham House stands on a promontory in a bend in the River Dart.
The sky clears. High cloud shadows race across field-carved crooked hills.
The very idea of the sea is hard to believe in, in rain and fog and dark.
A pair of swans swans about near the slipway at Blackness.
A half moon rises over Dittisham. We row down for a half at Ferry Boat Inn.
There are egrets, no regrets on the River Dart.
This is an achingly beautiful place to come across a little death.

J.R. Carpenter A walk through the Sharpham woods to Ashsprington point revealed that there are egrets yet no regrets on the River Dart.
27 August 2009 at 17:23 · Comment · Like

Lesley Johnson and Christine Wilks like this.

Christine Wilks :)))))
27 August 2009 at 19:12 · Delete

Carolyn Guertin Are you ever coming home?
27 August 2009 at 22:16 · Delete

Write a comment...

J.R. Carpenter It rained sideways all day in Devon, until we ventured out to pillage the orchard for plums. Then sky above the crooked hill field cleared.
26 August 2009 at 22:00 · Comment · Like

Kate Pullinger poured poured poured in Edinburgh...
26 August 2009 at 22:09 · Delete

J.R. Carpenter brilliant sunny Sunny Sunday in London - hope you have great weather out west.
26 August 2009 at 22:10 · Delete

Write a comment...

I've died and gone to Devon.
Mist moving over Dartmoor manages to make raw granite tor look ephemeral.
How does rain on magnolia leaves produce a dry, rustling sound?
We brave the rain to raid the orchard. Wet plums fall into waiting hands.
A pair of swans swans about near the slipway at Blackness.
Don't laugh at the Caution Slipway May Be Slippery sign. It may be true.
This is an achingly beautiful place to come across a little death.

I've died and gone to Devon.
Sharpham House stands on a promontory in a bend in the River Dart.
Meanders, bends in the river, don't last forever, but this house might.
It's so quiet here at night. The slightest sound carries.
The sea floats above a wave of hills, a thin strip bluer than the sky.
The fields get so muddy it's no wonder all the cows around here are brown.
This is an achingly beautiful place to come across a little death.

I've died and gone to Devon.
The three-hour drive from Heathrow to the West Country really takes four.
The deeper into Devon you drive, the narrower and more winding the roads.
In North America, roads this narrow wouldn't even count as driveways.
If this is the wrong side of the road, I don't care what's right.
The vineyard is full-moon-lit. It's impossible not to walk through it.
BBQs in Devon are just like BBQs in Nova Scotia: eventually it rains.
Flotsam on a tidal river is a strange mixture of oak leaves and seaweed.
This is an achingly beautiful place to come across a little death.

J.R. Carpenter How does rain on magnolia leaves produce this dry, rustling sound?
30 August 2009 at 18:58 · Comment · Like

J.R. Carpenter Breakfasted in a 16th c house in Totnes w. 1 Dalmatian, 2 eggs & 3 cakes. Recovering in an 18th c country house w. 1 novel & 1 long nap.
30 August 2009 at 14:14 · Comment · Like

Julie Mahfood likes this.

Write a comment...

J.R. Carpenter Damn. Now I'll want a row down the Dart in a Sandolo for a quick half at Ferry Boat Inn as the half moon rises over Dittisham every evening.
29 August 2009 at 22:01 · Comment · Like

Christine Wilks likes this.

Stephen Lawson and did some PInk come with it????
inquiring minds want to know...
29 August 2009 at 22:26 · Delete

J.R. Carpenter A bit brisk for Pink on the river so sipping Talisker back at the house.
29 August 2009 at 22:46 · Delete

Write a comment...

I've died and gone to Devon.
Mist moving over Dartmoor manages to make raw granite tor look ephemeral.
Cumulus sheep graze the high hill across from the house.
The vineyard is full-moon-lit. It's impossible not to walk through it.
From the lower drive, a view of the Dart opens north to Totnes.
The fields get so muddy it's no wonder the cows around here are brown.
The need for high-gloss violet Wellingtons soon becomes overwhelming.
A pair of swans swans about near the slipway at Blackness.
Don't laugh at the Caution Slipway May Be Slippery sign. It may be true.
This is an achingly beautiful place to come across a little death.

I've died and gone to Devon.
In North America, roads this narrow wouldn't even count as driveways.
How does rain on magnolia leaves produce a dry, rustling sound?.
Cumulus sheep graze the high hill across from the house.
The vineyard is full-moon-lit. It's impossible not to walk through it.
Totnes is pronounced like Loch Ness, only the monster is silent.
The fields get so muddy it's no wonder the cows around here are brown.
Cormorants line the riverbank, great wings hanging like laundry to dry.
There are egrets, no regrets on the River Dart.
This is an achingly beautiful place to come across a little death.

I've died and gone to Devon.
If this is the driveway, then I can't wait to see the house.
Sharpham House stands on a promontory in a bend in the River Dart.
It's an hour's walk to Totnes, along the Dart Valley footpath.
Totnes is pronounced like Loch Ness, only the monster is silent.
Fish & Chips taste best by the seaside. Same goes for crab sandwiches.
It's solid black night until late moonlight proves the vast water.
The fields get so muddy it's no wonder all the cows around here are brown.
Cormorants line the riverbank, great wings hanging like laundry to dry.
This is an achingly beautiful place to come across a little death.

J.R. Carpenter Thought the Dartmouth in Devon is livelier, prettier and much older than the one in Nova Scotia, both mouths open to the sea.
05 September 2009 at 19:27 · Comment · Like

J.R. Carpenter I thought nothing could top tonight's dinner until we walked through the full-moon-lit vineyard down to the hoot owl haunted high-tide river
04 September 2009 at 22:04 · Comment · Like

Shannon McPhee Sounds like romance to me!
04 September 2009 at 22:06 · Delete

Sandra Margolian I want to be there now.
04 September 2009 at 23:03 · Delete

Stephen Lawson glorious! moon-lit vineyard post wine with dinner I hope? and haunted owl on the plate?! very excited to hear how the evening ends (tho we can only guess with such cavorting amongst the full moon and tides!) We shall have to ask lady moon when she appears over here for gossip...
xxx
04 September 2009 at 23:36 · Delete

J.R. Carpenter the evening ends with three teenage girls descending on the house for a sleep over. lots of fifteen-year-old squeals and giggles downstairs, lots of ten-year-old Talisker consumed upstairs, and another very late night walk with the moon high over the crooked hills.
05 September 2009 at 12:44 · Delete

Emilie O'Brien double wow. :):)
05 September 2009 at 18:04 · Delete

Amanda J Kelly hoot owl haunted high-tide river
mmm
06 September 2009 at 17:10 · Delete

J.R. Carpenter by day it's nice to gander at the geese, but at night the owls really take over.
06 September 2009 at 17:28 · Delete

Write a comment...

I've died and gone to Devon.
The three-hour drive from Heathrow to the West Country really takes four.
Sharpham House stands on a promontory in a bend in the River Dart.
The vineyard is full-moon-lit. It's impossible not to walk through it.
The sky clears. High cloud shadows race across field-carved crooked hills.
Fish & Chips taste best by the seaside. Same goes for crab sandwiches.
A pair of swans swans about near the slipway at Blackness.
The fields get so muddy it's no wonder all the cows around here are brown.
This is an achingly beautiful place to come across a little death.

I've died and gone to Devon.
We can't hear the river from the house, but we can see it.
We brave the rain to raid the orchard. Wet plums fall into waiting hands.
On a clear day, from the top of the drive we can see south to the sea.
I lie awake thinking about the Dart carving its path through the night.
The Dart runs from Dartmoor, south to open its muddy mouth to the sea.
Everybody insists we're by the seaside. I can smell but not see the sea.
Flotsam on a tidal river is a strange mixture of oak leaves and seaweed.
This is an achingly beautiful place to come across a little death.

I've died and gone to Devon.
Sharpham House stands on a promontory in a bend in the River Dart.
We brave the rain to raid the orchard. Wet plums fall into waiting hands.
From the lower drive, a view of the Dart opens north to Totnes.
The fields get so muddy it's no wonder the cows around here are brown.
Everybody insists we're by the seaside. I can smell but not see the sea.
There are egrets, no regrets on the River Dart.
This is an achingly beautiful place to come across a little death.

I've died and gone to Devon.
England is a small country, unless you're driving across it.
In North America, roads this narrow wouldn't even count as driveways.
Sharpham House stands on a promontory in a bend in the River Dart.
We brave the rain to raid the orchard. Wet plums fall into waiting hands.
On a clear day, from the top of the drive we can see south to the sea.
It's an hour's walk to Totnes, along the Dart Valley footpath.
Fish & Chips taste best by the seaside. Same goes for crab sandwiches.
Don't laugh at the Caution Slipway May Be Slippery sign. It may be true.
This is an achingly beautiful place to come across a little death.

J.R. Carpenter Everybody insisted we were eating fish & chips by the seaside last night. I didn't believe it until late moonlight proved there was water.
09 September 2009 at 13:03 · Comment · Like

Naomi Charron For a second I thought you didn't believe you were eating fish and chips and I thought England zapped your tastebuds.
09 September 2009 at 13:42 · Delete

Write a comment...

RECENT ACTIVITY

J.R. wrote on Kate Pullinger's Wall.

J.R. attended "Textual Landscapes: Real and Imagined" at Bryce Wolkowitz gallery. · Comment · Like

J.R. and Patsy Van Roost are now friends. · Comment · Like

J.R. commented on Michael Stevenson's link.

J.R. Carpenter Mentally preparing to put the better part of the past 19 years of my life into storage: http://preview.tinyurl.com/klfhp5
08 September 2009 at 15:17 · Comment · Like

J.R. Carpenter It's so quiet here at night. The slightest sound carries. Owl calls over the river echo like drunken goodbyes hollered across 4am streets.
08 September 2009 at 06:03 · Comment · Like

J.R. Carpenter The ripe plums fall from the branches into your hands. If you happen to climb the fence and down the steep slope to raid the tree, that is.
06 September 2009 at 17:03 · Comment · Like

Julie Mahfood likes this.

Michael Stevenson I'm sorry, where the hell are you?
07 September 2009 at 01:42 · Delete

I've died and gone to Devon.
From the M3/A303 you'd think the whole country was countryside.
It's so quiet here at night. The slightest sound carries.
On a clear day, from the top of the drive we can see south to the sea.
The sea floats above a wave of hills, a thin strip bluer than the sky.
The very idea of the sea is hard to believe in, in rain and fog and dark.
It's solid black night until late moonlight proves the vast water.
A half moon rises over Dittisham. We row down for a half at Ferry Boat Inn.
The fields get so muddy it's no wonder all the cows around here are brown.
This is an achingly beautiful place to come across a little death.

I've died and gone to Devon.
A full moon whitewashes the hoot-owl-haunted high-tide river.
At low tide, stippled water scuds over mud-rucked sheets.
The vineyard is full-moon-lit. It's impossible not to walk through it.
On a clear day, from the top of the drive we can see south to the sea.
The Dart runs from Dartmoor, south to open its muddy mouth to the sea.
The fields get so muddy it's no wonder the cows around here are brown.
The very idea of the sea is hard to believe in, in rain and fog and dark.
Flotsam on a tidal river is a strange mixture of oak leaves and seaweed.
This is an achingly beautiful place to come across a little death.

I've died and gone to Devon.
The vineyard is full-moon-lit. It's impossible not to walk through it.
The sea floats above a wave of hills, a thin strip bluer than the sky.
It's an hour's walk to Totnes, along the Dart Valley footpath.
On rainy days someone always says: A little rain never hurt anyone.
The sky clears. High cloud shadows race across field-carved crooked hills.
A pair of swans swans about near the slipway at Blackness.
Cormorants line the riverbank, great wings hanging like laundry to dry.
This is an achingly beautiful place to come across a little death.

I've died and gone to Devon.
If this is the wrong side of the road, I don't care what's right.
A full moon whitewashes the hoot-owl-haunted high-tide river.
How does rain on magnolia leaves produce a dry, rustling sound?
The Dart runs from Dartmoor, south to open its muddy mouth to the sea.
There are egrets, no regrets on the River Dart.
This is an achingly beautiful place to come across a little death.

I've died and gone to Devon.
If this is the wrong side of the road, I don't care what's right.
Sharpham House stands on a promontory in a bend in the River Dart.
Totnes is pronounced like Loch Ness, only the monster is silent.
The need for high-gloss violet Wellingtons soon becomes overwhelming.
The very idea of the sea is hard to believe in, in rain and fog and dark.
Cormorants line the riverbank, great wings hanging like laundry to dry.
There are egrets, no regrets on the River Dart.
This is an achingly beautiful place to come across a little death.

J.R. Carpenter Totnes is pronounced like Loch Ness except the monster is silent.

27 October 2009 at 11:24 · Comment · Like

Emilie O'Brien, Caitlin Hartnett and 2 others like this.

Michael Boyce the monster is always silent until it comes out from under your bed

27 October 2009 at 18:58 · Delete

Corey Frost I visited Totnes once many years ago, and then walked 20 miles or so across Dartmoor and collapsed at a pub. Apparently my great great great grandfather was from Devon, and if you spend some time in both places you'll see there are striking resemblances between Devon and Prince Edward Island, in the names, in the landscape, in the color of the cliffs.

28 October 2009 at 01:18 · Delete

Write a comment...

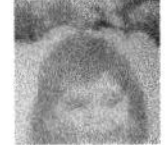

Elisabeth Belliveau omg j.r. - agatha christie's summer mansion is like 15k down the dart river from here... wanna go for a swim tomorrow?

27 October 2009 at 01:01 · Comment · Like · See Wall-to-Wall

J.R. Carpenter we've rowed past it. it's very yellow and lemon cake like.

27 October 2009 at 11:08 · Delete

Carolyn Guertin Apparently she ate a lot of apples in the bath while writing. Red, or green, apples? Lemon cake? Sounds like a colourful food mystery theme.

29 October 2009 at 00:38 · Delete

Write a comment...

I've died and gone to Devon.
Sharpham House stands on a promontory in a bend in the River Dart.
How does rain on magnolia leaves produce a dry, rustling sound?
We wade through Wellington tall grasses hunting for fallen walnuts.
On a clear day, from the top of the drive we can see south to the sea.
There are egrets, no regrets on the River Dart.
This is an achingly beautiful place to come across a little death.

I've died and gone to Devon.
Meanders, bends in the river, don't last forever, but this house might.
We wade through Wellington tall grasses hunting for fallen walnuts.
From the lower drive, a view of the Dart opens north to Totnes.
BBQs in Devon are just like BBQs in Nova Scotia: eventually it rains.
The fields get so muddy it's no wonder all the cows around here are brown.
This is an achingly beautiful place to come across a little death.

I've died and gone to Devon.
We can't hear the river from the house, but we can see it.
It's so quiet here at night. The slightest sound carries.
How does rain on magnolia leaves produce a dry, rustling sound?.
We wade through Wellington tall grasses hunting for fallen walnuts.
The need for high-gloss violet Wellingtons soon becomes overwhelming.
The very idea of the sea is hard to believe in, in rain and fog and dark.
A half moon rises over Dittisham. We row down for a half at Ferry Boat Inn.
Flotsam on a tidal river is a strange mixture of oak leaves and seaweed.
There are egrets, no regrets on the River Dart.
This is an achingly beautiful place to come across a little death.

J.R. Carpenter It's rush hour at the rookery, a mass of black birds swirling over the high ridge of Sharpham Wood.
30 October 2009 at 18:26 · Comment · Like

J.R. Carpenter Striding across the English countryside wearing high gloss violet wellinningtons, surely world domination will soon be within reach.

Original Gloss « Original « Catalogue « Hunter Boots
www.hunter-boot.com
Upper : Vulcanised natural rubber construction, built on an orthopaedic last for the legendary Hunter fit. High gloss finish

30 October 2009 at 13:25 · Comment · Like · Share

Alice van der Klei, Meg Nolia and Nora Pierce like this.

Dana Bath I just bought a pair of these boots! The violet ones! They are fantastic, but more appropriate and useful in Vancouver, where I bought them, than here in Montreal.
30 October 2009 at 14:57 · Delete

J.R. Carpenter If you aren't finding enough occasions to wear your wellingtons in Montreal, I totally recommend moving to the English countryside. It's muddy and green, always wet, and there are public foot paths everywhere, for walking picturesquely across fields.
30 October 2009 at 16:04 · Delete

Michael Boyce sounds awesome!
30 October 2009 at 19:42 · Delete

Valérie D. Walker love the muddly paths!
30 October 2009 at 23:43 · Delete

Dream Listener we used to call those things gum boots...
31 October 2009 at 01:43 · Delete

Write a comment...

I've died and gone to Devon.
From the M3/A303 you'd think the whole country was countryside.
Meanders, bends in the river, don't last forever, but this house might.
How does English optimism turn mostly cloudy into sunny intervals?
It's an hour's walk to Totnes, along the Dart Valley footpath.
I lie awake thinking about the Dart carving its path through the night.
The Dart runs from Dartmoor, south to open its muddy mouth to the sea.
The need for high-gloss violet Wellingtons soon becomes overwhelming.
It's solid black night until late moonlight proves the vast water.
This is an achingly beautiful place to come across a little death.

I've died and gone to Devon.
England is a small country, unless you're driving across it.
The three-hour drive from Heathrow to the West Country really takes four.
If this is the driveway, then I can't wait to see the house.
Sharpham House stands on a promontory in a bend in the River Dart.
How does rain on magnolia leaves produce a dry, rustling sound?
How does English optimism turn mostly cloudy into sunny intervals?
Flotsam on a tidal river is a strange mixture of oak leaves and seaweed.
This is an achingly beautiful place to come across a little death.

J.R. Carpenter Lying awake thinking about the river carving its path through the night.

15 November 2009 at 05:52 · Comment · Like

Amanda J Kelly for some reason i imagine if you're thinking about it you can hear it and the thought of the sound of a river makes me happy today... thanks!

15 November 2009 at 20:01 · Delete

Linda Dornan I went for a walk by the ocean yesterday, the sound and smell makes me happy, too.

15 November 2009 at 21:50 · Delete

J.R. Carpenter I can't hear the river from the house, but I can see it. there were gale force winds and rain for two days. when they stopped in the night it was suddenly so silent it woke me and for a long time all I could think of was the river

15 November 2009 at 22:09 · Delete

Write a comment...

J.R. Carpenter No getting out of Sharpham today. We have a flat tired & gale force winds brought a great beech down across the top of the drive.

14 November 2009 at 12:42 · Comment · Like

I’ve died and gone to Devon.
It’s so quiet here at night. The slightest sound carries.
Meanders, bends in the river, don’t last forever, but this house might.
A full moon whitewashes the hoot-owl-haunted high-tide river.
How does rain on magnolia leaves produce a dry, rustling sound?
I lie awake thinking about the Dart carving its path through the night.
Flotsam on a tidal river is a strange mixture of oak leaves and seaweed.
This is an achingly beautiful place to come across a little death.

SOURCE CODE: Devon.py

```
#!//usr/bin/python
#Story generation by Nick Montfort
#Story by J.R. Carpenter
#2009-11-11
from random import choice
while True:
 s=['England is a small country, unless you\'re driving across it',
  'The three-hour drive from Heathrow to the West Country really takes four',
  'From the M3/A303 you\'d think the whole country was countryside',
  'Mist moving over Dartmoor manages to make raw granite tor look ephemeral',
  'The deeper into Devon you drive, the narrower and more winding the roads',
  'In North America, roads this narrow wouldn\'t even count as driveways',
  'If this is the wrong side of the road, I don\'t care what\'s right',
  'If this is the driveway, then I can\'t wait to see the house',
  'Sharpham House stands on a promontory in a bend in the River Dart',
  'Meanders, bends in the river, don\'t last forever, but this house might',
  'We can\'t hear the river from the house, but we can see it',
  'It\'s so quiet here at night. The slightest sound carries',
  'A full moon whitewashes the hoot-owl-haunted high-tide river',
  'At low tide, stippled water scuds over mud-rucked sheets',
  'How does rain on magnolia leaves produce a dry, rustling sound?',
  'How does English optimism turn mostly cloudy into sunny intervals?',
  'Cumulus sheep graze the high hill across from the house',
  'The vineyard is full-moon-lit. It\'s impossible not to walk through it',
  'We wade through Wellington tall grasses hunting for fallen walnuts',
  'We brave the rain to raid the orchard. Wet plums fall into waiting hands',
  'Free range rabbits hide in blackberry brambles rambling along the river',
  'On a clear day, from the top of the drive we can see south to the sea',
  'The sea floats above a wave of hills, a thin strip bluer than the sky',
  'From the lower drive, a view of the Dart opens north to Totnes',
  'It\'s an hour\'s walk to Totnes, along the Dart Valley footpath',
  'Totnes is pronounced like Loch Ness, only the monster is silent',
  'Dartmouth, Devon, is 98% prettier than Dartmouth, Nova Scotia',
  'I lie awake thinking about the Dart carving its path through the night',
  'The Dart runs from Dartmoor, south to open its muddy mouth to the sea',
  'BBQs in Devon are just like BBQs in Nova Scotia: eventually it rains',
```

```
 'On rainy days someone always says: A little rain never hurt anyone',
 'The sky clears. High cloud shadows race across field-carved crooked hills',
 'The fields get so muddy it\'s no wonder the cows around here are brown',
 'The need for high-gloss violet Wellingtons soon becomes overwhelming',
 'Fish & Chips taste best by the seaside. Same goes for crab sandwiches',
 'Everybody insists we\'re by the seaside. I can smell but not see the sea',
 'The very idea of the sea is hard to believe in, in rain and fog and dark',
 'It\'s solid black night until late moonlight proves the vast water',
 'A pair of swans swans about near the slipway at Blackness',
 'Don\'t laugh at the Caution Slipway May Be Slippery sign. It may be true',
 'A half moon rises over Dittisham. We row down for a half at Ferry Boat Inn',
 'Flotsam on a tidal river is a strange mixture of oak leaves and seaweed',
 'The fields get so muddy it\'s no wonder all the cows around here are brown',
 'Cormorants line the riverbank, great wings hanging like laundry to dry',
 'There are egrets, no regrets on the River Dart']
l=choice(range(5,10))
while len(s)>l:
 s.remove(choice(s))
print "\nI've died and gone to Devon.\n"+'.\n'.join(s)+'.'
raw_input('This is an achingly beautiful place to come across a little
death.')
```

DOWNLOAD: http://luckysoap.com/generation/Devon.zip

Download the python file to your desktop and unzip. On a Mac or Linux system, you can run the story generator by opening a Terminal Window, typing "cd Desktop", and typing "python Devon.py". Hint: look for Terminal in your Utilities folder. These Python story generator runs on Windows, too, but you will probably need to install Python first: http://www.python.org/download/releases/2.6.5/. Once Python is installed, double click on the file and it will automatically launch and run in a terminal window. Every time you press ENTER a new version of the story will appear.

J.R. Carpenter going to the seaside to see the sea
22 November 2009 at 14:22 · Comment · Like

Sonia Thomson please do sell some sea shells.
22 November 2009 at 17:51 · Delete

J.R. Carpenter I was very tempted to wheel a wheelbarrow through streets wide and narrow singing cockles and mussels alive alive oh. but there were no streets wide, only narrow.
22 November 2009 at 18:41 · Delete

Nora Maynard how bout a beautiful pea-green boat?
22 November 2009 at 19:11 · Delete

J.R. Carpenter When the Walrus said, "The time has come to talk of many things," I brought up the subject of the beautiful pea-green boat, but he kept going on about shoes and ships and sealing-wax, cabbages and kings and why the sea is boiling hot and whether pigs have wings.
22 November 2009 at 19:30 · Delete

Nora Maynard ..if seven maids with seven mops swept it for half a year, do you suppose, the Walrus said, that they could get it clear?
22 November 2009 at 19:48 · Delete

J.R. Carpenter Wait, is one of those maids my Bonnie? My Bonnie lies over the ocean, and, if you've seen here, please bring back, bring back, bring back my Bonnie to me, to me.
24 November 2009 at 12:47 · Delete

Write a comment...

To See The Sea

On a clear day, and there aren't very many of those, from a spot at the top of the drive you can see south to the sea. This is confusing, because the sea appears to float above a wave of hills. A thin strip bluer than the sky.

Lower down the drive, a view of the River Dart opens north to Totnes. I would say this driveway boasts the best views in England, but so far it's the only driveway in England I'm familiar with.

Sometimes I lie awake and think about the river carving its path through the night, north to Totnes, south to Dartmouth; north to the Dartmoor, south to the sea.

Amanda said, For some reason I imagine if you're thinking about it you can hear it and the thought of the sound of a river makes me happy today.

Linda said, I went for a walk by the ocean yesterday, the sound and smell makes me happy, too.

I can't hear the river from the house, but I can see it from the bedroom. Last week there were gale force winds and rain for two days. When the storm stopped in the night the silence was so sudden it woke me. I lay awake and thought about the rain-swollen river opening its muddy mouth to the sea.

On Sunday I said, I'm going to the seaside to see the sea.

Sonia said, Please do sell some seashells.

I confessed to Sonia that I was sorely tempted to wheel a wheelbarrow through streets wide and narrow singing cockles and mussels alive alive oh. But, this being Devon, there were no streets wide, only narrow.

Nora said, How bout a beautiful pea-green boat?

There are Owls roosting all up and down the River Dart. But no Pussy-cats. And I am a Carpenter, after all. As such, I assured Nora, when the Walrus said, "The time has come to talk of many things," I immediately brought up the subject of the beautiful pea-green boat, but he kept going on about shoes and ships and sealing-wax, cabbages and kings and why the sea is boiling hot and whether pigs have wings.

I took a photo of Blackpool Sands, but it came out kind of dark. Possibly because the beach has black in its name. And, although the sun was shining on the sea, shining with all his might, this was odd, because it was the middle of the night.

The Walrus and I were wearing Wellingtons and walking close at hand; we wept like anything to see such quantities of sand.

Nora wondered, as did the Walrus, ..if seven maids with seven mops swept it for half a year, do you suppose that they could get it clear?

Wait, I said to Nora. Is one of those maids my Bonnie? My Bonnie lies over the ocean, and, if you've seen her, could you please bring back, bring back, bring back my Bonnie to me, to me?

The Bonnie bit may seem a bit tacked on after that Walrus and Carpenter bit, but Amanda, Linda, Sonia and Nora all lie over the ocean, and that's what made me think of it.

J.R. Carpenter

To See The Sea

On a clear day, and there aren't very many of those, from a spot at the top of the drive you can see south to the sea. This is confusing, because the sea appears to float above a wave of hills. A t...more

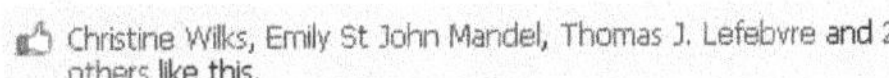

11 December 2009 at 21:29 · Comment · Like · Share it

Christine Wilks, Emily St John Mandel, Thomas J. Lefebvre and 2 others like this.

Emily St John Mandel I love this.
11 December 2009 at 23:43

J.R. Carpenter I love the conversations that happen between strangers in post comments. None of the friends named in this piece know each other, but their comments on a common theme connected some dots in my mind. I've got a River Dart specific Twitter feed going, if anyone's interested: http://twitter.com/TheRiverDart I'm re-tweeting bits from this piece right now, but it's mostly new writing toward a new e.lit project that will eventually pull in the above profile's RSS feed.
12 December 2009 at 12:59 · Delete

Write a comment...

THIRD GENERATION

Auto-Autobiography

"If you move around all your life, you can't find where you come from on a map. All those places where you lived are just that: places. You don't come from any of them; you come from a series of events. And those are mapped in memory. Contingent, precarious events, without the counterpane of place to muffle the knowledge of how unlikely we are. Almost not born at every turn. Without a place, events slow-tumbling through time become your roots. Stories shading into one another. You come from a plane crash. From a war that brought your parents together."

Anne-Marie MacDonald, *As The Crow Flies*

Here is my story:
I was born on a back-to-the-land farm.
I come from a series of events free-falling through time.
My mother was reading a murder mystery the night I was born.
I live within my means.
I work at this hair, it doesn't just happen.
I wish people still traveled by steamship.
My best friend kept insisting I learn to play guitar.
In retrospect, she didn't run from home. It was done by train.
I love it when the rooks fly back to the rookery, eerie-like.
Next year, let's get up less and less early each morning.
In future, we will know many beginnings and no ends.

Here is my story:
I was born on the night shift, nurses few and far between.
I come from a collection of places I can't find on a map.
My father dated a Phys. Ed. teacher once. It was exhausting.
I live somewhere that isn't going to last.
I work at blurring boundaries and confounding categories.
I wish I could get more excited about wishing.
My best friend had a penchant for impractical footwear.
In retrospect, she read way too many Russian novels.
I love it when someone comes up with a better plan than mine.
Next year, let's learn thousands of new of things.
In future, we will know many beginnings and no ends.

Here is my story:
I was born on a back-to-the-land farm.
I come from a war that brought my parents together.
My father dated a child psychologist once. What hell.
I live in a small flat in a small country.
I work toward graceful fails.
I wish all of the above were true.
My best friend was a tiny bit smarter than me.
In retrospect, she was the lesser of four or five evils.
I love it when deep-seated fears turn out to be unfounded.
Next year, let's learn thousands of new of things.
In future, we will know many beginnings and no ends.

Here is my story:
I was born in one of the less decorous centuries.
I come from the nothing that springs between small towns.
My mother dated a child psychologist once. What hell.
I live in love.
I work when I want to.
I wish we could stay here.
My best friend resented Montreal, and me for loving it.
In retrospect, he read way too many Russian novels.
I love it when we lie in bed plotting the downfall of our enemies.
Next year, let's file taxes separately.
In future, we will know many beginnings and no ends.

Here is my story:
I was born on a back-to-the-land farm.
I come from the forest primeval, according to Longfellow.
My father dated a postal worker once. And only once.
I live in a number of different pasts.
I work better when I have a deadline.
I wish I could get rid of this cold.
My best friend kept insisting I learn to play guitar.
In retrospect, she must have known vodka would end in heartache.
I love it when postcards arrive from far away places.
Next year, let's file taxes separately.
In future, we will know many beginnings and no ends.

Here is my story:
I was born before VCRs, DVDs or SUVs were invented.
I come from a land with no gravity, only levity.
My mother has humiliated me for the second-to-last time.
I live in a number of different pasts.
I work from home.
I wish all of the above were true.
My best friend was a tiny bit smarter than me.
In retrospect, she was the lesser of four or five evils.
I love it when things my mother told me turn out to be wrong.
Next year, let's forget every single thing we learned this year.
In future, we will know many beginnings and no ends.

Here is my story:
I was born before VCRs, DVDs or SUVs were invented.
I come from the forest primeval, according to Longfellow.
My mother had a long memory and a short fuse.
I live on potatoes, despite a love of all foods green.
I work hard at not having to work too hard.
I wish there were designated reading days.
My best friend resented Montreal, and me for loving it.
In retrospect, she proved spelling is totally irrelevant.
I love it when deep-seated fears turn out to be unfounded.
Next year, let's forget every single thing we learned this year.
In future, we will know many beginnings and no ends.

Here is my story:
I was born before VCRs, DVDs or SUVs were invented.
I come from a collection of places I can't find on a map.
My father and I haven't spoken for six blissful years.
I live somewhere that isn't going to last.
I work at blurring boundaries and confounding categories.
I wish for another wish plus one.
My best friend lived too far away for us to bother arguing.
In retrospect, she proved spelling is totally irrelevant.
I love it when someone comes up with a better plan than mine.
Next year, let's find different answers for these same questions.
In future, we will know many beginnings and no ends.

Here is my story:
I was born on a back-to-the-land farm.
I come from a collection of places I can't find on a map.
My father dated a Phys. Ed. teacher once. It was exhausting.
I live with a 15-year-old girl in a 250-year-old house.
I work to embrace vagaries.
I wish my books weren't in storage.
My best friend never knew when I was joking.
In retrospect, he read way too many Russian novels.
I love it when someone comes up with a better plan than mine.
Next year, let's file taxes separately.
In future, we will know many beginnings and no ends.

Here is my story:
I was born on a back-to-the-land farm.
I come from the nothing that springs between small towns.
My mother made me make all the decisions.
I live in jeans, flip-flops and tank-tops.
I work better when I have a deadline.
I wish I'd said that differently.
My best friend has yet to read my first novel.
In retrospect, he must have known vodka would end in heartache.
I love it when deep-seated fears turn out to be unfounded.
Next year, let's spend at least one day a week in Bristol.
In future, we will know many beginnings and no ends.

Here is my story:
I was born in a different country than anyone I'm related to.
I come from a long line of school teachers.
My father dated a Phys. Ed. teacher once. It was exhausting.
I live in a number of different pasts.
I work to embrace vagaries.
I wish I could remember the other half of French.
My best friend kept insisting I learn to play guitar.
In retrospect, she never wanted to buy a house.
I love it when we lie in bed plotting the downfall of our enemies.
Next year, let's row the boat down lots of different streams.
In future, we will know many beginnings and no ends.

Here is my story:
I was born in one of the less decorous centuries.
I come from a visual arts background.
My father made me make all the decisions.
I live an hour's walk from the nearest town.
I work better when I have a deadline.
I wish people still traveled by steamship.
My best friend kept insisting I learn to play guitar.
In retrospect, she didn't run from home. It was done by train.
I love it when the cows line up and start walking in a row.
Next year, let's face it – world domination will be within reach.
In future, we will know many beginnings and no ends.

Here is my story:
I was born on the night shift, nurses few and far between.
I come from far from wherever it is money comes from.
My father was pathologically insecure.
I live in a wonderful house.
I work at blurring boundaries and confounding categories.
I wish I could get more excited about wishing.
My best friend lived too far away for us to bother arguing.
In retrospect, she may have the best timing in the world.
I love it when the rooks fly back to the rookery, eerie-like.
Next year, let's forget every single thing we learned this year.
In future, we will know many beginnings and no ends.

Here is my story:
I was born before VCRs, DVDs or SUVs were invented.
I come from far away on the briny ocean's toss.
My mother was pathologically insecure.
I live in jeans, flip-flops and tank-tops.
I work to embrace vagaries.
I wish all of the above were true.
My best friend had a penchant for impractical footwear.
In retrospect, she didn't run from home. It was done by train.
I love it when the rooks fly back to the rookery, eerie-like.
Next year, let's learn thousands of new of things.
In future, we will know many beginnings and no ends.

Here is my story:
I was born in a different country than anyone I'm related to.
I come from the forest primeval, according to Longfellow.
My father was 22 when I was born, which seems too young to me.
I live within my means.
I work so slowly sometimes I forget what I'm working on.
I wish I wouldn't get so worked up over things.
My best friend was a tiny bit smarter than me.
In retrospect, she read way too many Russian novels.
I love it when someone comes up with a better plan than mine.
Next year, let's replace the windows.
In future, we will know many beginnings and no ends.

SOURCE CODE: autobio.py

```
#!/usr/bin/python
#AutoAutoBiography by J. R. Carpenter
#adapted from a script by Nick Montfort
#2010
from random import choice
born=['in a different country than anyone I\'m related to',
  'on the night shift, nurses few and far between',
  'on a back-to-the-land farm',
  'aloft by work worn hands, the whole room spinning',
  'in one of the less fashionable provinces',
  'in one of the less decorous centuries',
  'in the humid hum of a hay-sweet summer',
  'without memory',
  'in the calm before thunder that brought no rain',
  'before VCRs, DVDs or SUVs were invented',
  'in wedlock - for some reason, this surprises me',
  'in a town so small there wasn\'t even a hotel in it']
come=['the lower east side of a city I\'ve never lived in',
  'the nothing that springs between small towns',
  'the forest primeval, according to Longfellow',
  'a collection of places I can\'t find on a map',
  'a long line of school teachers',
  'a visual arts background',
  'far from wherever it is money comes from',
  'a land with no gravity, only levity',
  'a war that brought my parents together',
  'a series of events free-falling through time',
  'north of the North Mountain',
  'far away on the briny ocean\'s toss',
  'the North Mountain. Not the part you\'re thinking of']
parent=['left when I was eight and that\'s the good news',
  'and I haven\'t spoken for six blissful years',
  'was 22 when I was born, which seems too young to me',
   'made me make all the decisions',
  'was pathologically insecure',
  'was the least parented parent I\'ve ever met',
  'was reading a murder mystery the night I was born',
  'had a long memory and a short fuse',
  'has humiliated me for the second-to-last time',
  'would climb up on the cross for my brother',
  'dated a child psychologist once. What hell',
  'dated a postal worker once. And only once',
```

```
  'dated a Phys. Ed. teacher once. It was exhausting']
live=['in a small flat in a small country',
  'an hour\'s walk from the nearest town',
  'on a promontory in a bend in the River Dart',
  'in love',
  'on potatoes, despite a love of all foods green',
  'with a 15-year-old girl in a 250-year-old year old house',
  'somewhere that isn\'t going to last',
  'in a number of different pasts',
  'in jeans, flip-flops and tank-tops',
  'with my mother\'s insecurities',
  'in rural splendour',
  'within my means',
  'in a constant state of interruption',
  'to live, not to be remembered',
  'in a wonderful house',
  'in my head']
work=['from home',
  'hardest on my own projects',
  'with what I have',
  'when I want to',
  'best from bed, books and phone within reach',
  'on lots of things at once',
  'from home',
  'to embrace vagaries',
  'better when I have a deadline',
  'with found materials',
  'hard at not having to work too hard',
   'at blurring boundaries and confounding categories',
  'at this hair, it doesn\'t just happen',
  'so slowly sometimes I forget what I\'m working on',
    'toward graceful fails']
friend=['kept insisting I learn to play guitar',
  'convinced me seafood really is food',
  'gave me Borges to read and Bach to listen to',
  'was a tiny bit smarter than me',
  'has yet to read my first novel',
  'lent me a shower curtain, no questions asked',
  'had a penchant for impractical footwear',
  'lived too far away for us to bother arguing',
  'dumped me for a rocket scientist',
  'never knew when I was joking',
  'kept smoking just quit doing it in front of me',
  'resented Montreal, and me for loving it',
  'moved to Vancouver when I wasn\'t looking']
retrospect=['read way too many Russian novels',
```

```
  'may have the best timing in the world',
   'was speaking a separate language',
  'never wanted to buy a house',
   'was the lesser of four or five evils',
  'rarely convinced me of anything',
  'proved spelling is totally irrelevant',
  'was a little too good a keeping secrets',
  'must have known vodka would end in heartache',
  'didn\'t run from home. It was done by train']
wish=['it would stop raining',
  'we had floor-to-ceiling bookcases',
  'I could get more excited about wishing',
  'I could get rid of this cold',
  'wishes came true',
  'things were simpler',
  'I could fall asleep',
  'people still traveled by steamship',
  'I\'d said that differently',
  'we could stay here',
  'everyone could personalize their own weather',
  'all of the above were true',
  'for another wish plus one',
  'my books weren\'t in storage',
  'there were designated reading days',
  'I wouldn\'t get so worked up over things',
  'I could remember the other half of French']
love=['we lie in bed plotting the downfall of our enemies',
  'postcards arrive from far away places',
  'the cows line up and start walking in a row',
  'someone comes up with a better plan than mine',
  'things my mother told me turn out to be wrong',
  'deep-seated fears turn out to be unfounded',
  'the moon is bright enough to read by',
  'the rooks fly back to the rookery, eerie-like']
nextyear=['pick sloe berries down by the river',
  'spend at least one day a week in Bristol',
  'replace the windows',
   'face it - world domination will be within reach',
  'write more books',
   'find different answers for these same questions',
  'buy a printer',
  'hope things are exactly as they are now',
  'get up less and less early each morning',
  'go to Paris, Vienna and New York, in that order',
  'learn thousands of new of things',
   'forget every single thing we learned this year',
```

```
  'go somewhere cold in the winter',
  'row the boat down lots of different streams',
  'file taxes separately']
while True:
 print "\nHere is my story:\n""I was born "+choice(born)+'.\n'"I
come from "+choice(come)+'.\n'+choice(['My mother','My father']),
choice(parent)+'.\n'"I live "+choice(live)+'.\n'"I work
"+choice(work)+'.\n'"I wish "+choice(wish)+'.\n'"My best friend
"+choice(friend)+'.\n'"In retrospect, "+choice(['he ','she '])
+choice(retrospect)+'.\n'"I love it when "+choice(love)+'.\n'"Next year,
let\'s "+choice(nextyear)+'.'
 raw_input('In future, we will know many beginnings and no ends.')
```

DOWNLOAD: http://luckysoap.com/generations/autobio.zip

Download the python file to your desktop and unzip. On a Mac or Linux system, you can run the story generator by opening a Terminal Window, typing "cd Desktop", and typing "python autobio.py". Hint: look for Terminal in your Utilities folder. These Python story generator runs on Windows, too, but you will probably need to install Python first: http://www.python.org/download/releases/2.6.5/. Once Python is installed, double click on the file and it will automatically launch and run in a terminal window. Every time you press ENTER a new version of the story will appear.

At 07:05 PM 15/05/2010, Scott Rettberg wrote:

A Saturday amusement for you. A hacking of a hacking -- JRs remix of one of Nick's story generators. I turned JRs autobiography generator into a compulsion narrative generator.

To run, control click and open with Python launcher. Hit return to compulsively generate a new story.

All the Best,

Scott

```
#!/usr/bin/python
#AutoCompulsion by Scott Rettberg
#Overwritten from AutoAutoBiography by J. R. Carpenter
#adapted from script by Nick Montfort
#2010
```

FOURTH GENERATION

Gorge

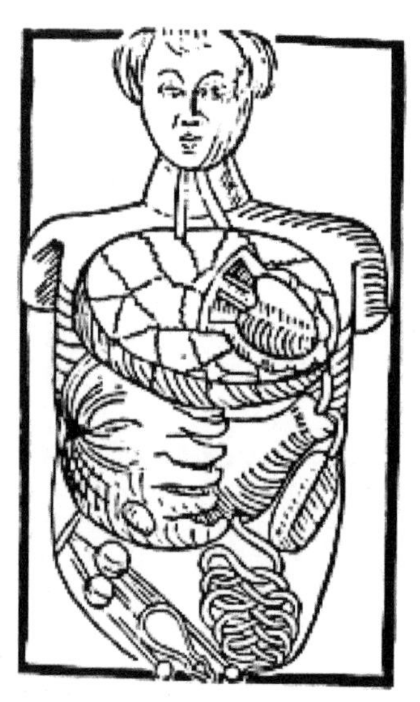

Gorge distils the morsel.
Sweat singes the bowels.

write the burnt cordial liquor –

Craving ripens the slightest sliver.
Gullets balance.
Dressings steep.
Digestive juices melt the thick spreads.

obliterate the blackstrap burnt cardamom –

Digestive juice distils the vein.
Flared nostrils marinate.
Dressings absorb.
Glaze distils the most intimate odour.

release the berry blackstrap ginger –

Mandibles stain the morsel.
Smells skin the meal.

examine the cinnamon –

Gazes ingest the morsel.
Gazes mature.
Thick spreads soak.
Nose weakens the flushed cheeks.

scrutinize the almond cassis cordial liquorice –

Maw skims the lower lip.
Palms reduce.
Flushed cheeks layer.
Enzymes drive the thick spread.

become the cassis –

Gorges split the meal.
Most intimate odours savour.
Spits engage the bowel.

gorge on the cassis -

Brains pick the thick spreads.
Heads brew.
Intellects pluck the proffered finger.

decant the blackstrap cassis colourful aftertaste –

Glazes ink the bowls.
Spits brew.
Vinaigrettes dissolve.
Thirst dissects the bowls.

read the barely perceptible cinnamon colourful cordial –

Knowledge picks the pores.
Minds incorporate.
Sight singes the taste bud.

inhabit the cordial ginger –

Muscle weakens the vein.
Digestive tracts cool.
Gaze ripens the veins.

examine the damson herbaceous –

Throat dissects the blood vessel.
Soft pockets mature.
Thirsts age.

Throats grate the flushed cheeks.

sip the cinnamon citrus liquor aftertaste –

Knowledge melts the flared nostrils.
Mouths julienne the dips.

observe the blackstrap cassis –

Brain incises the tongue.
Maws warm.
Sweats carve the persistent scents.

savour the rich ginger –

Appetites texture the guts.
Knowledges brew.
Muscle attracts the stomachs.

translate the cinnamon liquorice –

Smells sever the soft pocket.
Craving boils the vein.

slice the faint burnt ginger liquorice –

Digestive juice weakens the membrane.
Pores soak.
Slightest slivers sip.
Molars carve the vein.

decant the herbaceous –

Brain distils the vinaigrettes.
Enzymes braise the proffered finger.

note the almond cassis –

Nose devours the morsel.
Vinaigrettes steep.
Incisor distils the film.

study the cinnamon cordial –

Gorges wilt the lower lip.
Knowledges round.
Films incorporate.
Maw engages the tongues.

slice the cassis –

Gorge agitates the proffered finger.
Soft pockets complement.
Language stirs the slightest slivers.

write the almond blackstrap burnt cinnamon –

Mind yields the surface.
Incisors sip.
Spit bites the bowel.

release the berry citrus –

Maws distil the bowels.
Nose splits the dressings.

examine the blackstrap –

Gullets strengthen the soft pockets.
Dressings encrust.
Surfaces brew.
Incisors yield the morsel.

examine the colourful herbaceous liquorice aftertaste –

Jaw grinds the blood vessels.
Gazes fill the soft pockets.

write the cardamom cinnamon –

Smell carves the lips.
Lower lips mature.
Gorges consume the stomachs.

translate the aftertaste –

Incisors drink the vinaigrettes.
Smells incise the morsels.

study the blackstrap ginger aftertaste –

Intellects whip the bowels.
Dressings reduce.
Language fills the dressings.

write the smoky berry cordial herbaceous –

Muscle devours the finger tips.
Gorges ink the soft pockets.

examine the almond cinnamon ginger –

Sweats distil the thick spread.
Mandibles complement.
Gazes consume the most intimate odour.

write the blackstrap ginger liquorice aftertaste –

Gazes split the film.
Sights fill the film.

release the citrus cordial –

Spits ripen the lower lips.
Aromas absorb.
Cravings soak.
Languages pick the vinaigrette.

confuse the burnt cordial –

Glaze agitates the dips.
Cravings complement.
Knowledges peel the persistent scent.

examine the burnt cardamom ginger liquor –

Intellects char the palms.
Blood vessels layer.
Bladders brew.
Spits strain the thick spread.

write the almond cardamom damson aftertaste –

Thirsts julienne the bowl.
Spirit engages the crusts.

confuse the almond burnt cassis damson –

Intellect tears the aroma.
Crusts encrust.
Pores warm.
Intellects distil the stomachs.

note the cautious colourful herbaceous –

Gorges digest the aromas.
Enzymes cream.
Gaze drives the bowls.

savour the almond berry –

Molars savour.
Maw fills the membrane.

scrutinize the blackstrap cinnamon –

Digestive juices strengthen the films.
Palms layer.
Persistent scents concentrate.
Sweats dominate the slightest sliver.

translate the supple cassis cordial aftertaste –

Spit coats the slightest sliver.
Morsels sip.
Aromas round.
Gaze whips the slightest sliver.

obliterate the blackstrap cordial liquorice –

Appetite whips the veins.
Palms balance.
Finger tips steep.
Gaze ingests the palm.

examine the cassis –

Maws direct the membrane.
Muscle coats the sauce.

gorge on the dense almond citrus cordial –

Noses melt the bladder.
Most intimate odours warm.
Membranes mature.
Sight coats the meal.

release the almond blackstrap –

Meals steam.
Sight cracks the morsel.

obliterate the blackstrap cardamom ginger liquor –

Digestive tracts texture the dressing.
Jaw strengthens the flushed cheeks.

scrutinize the colourful cordial –

Sight braises the pores.
Gullet stimulates the persistent scents.

observe the berry colourful damson ginger –

Digestive juice styles the taste buds.
Appetite stuffs the guts.

inhabit the burnt liquor –

Desires grind the soft pocket.
Vinaigrettes steep.
Mandible carves the meals.

observe the blackstrap –

Gaze inks the bladder.
Spirits ripen.
Vinaigrettes complement.
Knowledge engages the finger tip.

inhabit the cardamom ginger herbaceous liquorice –

Sight chews the soft pockets.
Flared nostrils assimilate.
Most intimate odours dissolve.
Sights sever the dressings.

gorge on the berry citrus aftertaste –

Jaws ingest the dressings.
Gorge ripens the flared nostrils.

LAPSUS LINGUAE, May 26, 2010:

GORGE

A gorge is a steep-sided canyon, a passage, a gullet. To gorge is to stuff with food, to devour greedily. GORGE is a new poetry generator by J. R. Carpenter. This never-ending tract spews verse approximations, poetic paroxysms on food, consumption, decadence and desire.

The source code for GORGE is a hack of Nick Montfort's elegant poetry generator Taroko Gorge, which has also been remixed by Scott Rettberg, as Tokyo Garage.

Of GORGE, Nick Montfort advises:

> "See if you can stomach it, and for how long."
>
> Nick Montfort, Post Position, *Once More into the Gorge* http://nickm.com/post/2010/05/once-more-into-the-gorge/

http://luckysoap.com/lapsuslinguae/2010/05/gorge/

SOURCE CODE: http://luckysoap.com/generation/gorge.html

```
<!DOCTYPE html PUBLIC "-//W3C//DTD HTML 4.01 Transitional//EN">
<html>
<head>
<meta http-equiv="content-type" content="text/html; charset=utf-8">
 <title>GORGE || J. R. Carpenter</title>
 <!-- a remix of Taroko Gorge, by Nick Montfort http://nickm.com/poems/
taroko_gorge.html -->
<style type="text/css">
/* <![CDATA[ */
body {background: #cccccc; color: #cc0033; margin: 0 24pt 0 24pt; font-
family: Optima, sans-serif; font-size: 13pt;}
div {height: 16pt;}
a {color: #117; text-decoration: none;}
/* ]]> */
</style>
<script language="JavaScript" type="text/javascript">
var t=0;
var n=0;
var paths=0;
var above='appetite,brain,craving,desire,digestive juice,digestive
tract,enzyme,gaze,glaze,gorge,gullet,head,incisor,intellect,jaw,
knowledge,language,maw,mandible,mind,molar,muscle,mouth,nose,
passion, sight,smell,spit,sweat,spirit,thirst,throat'.split(',');
var below='aroma,bladder,blood vessel,bowl,bowel,crust,dip,dressing,
film,gut,lip,lower lip,proffered finger,finger tip,flared nostril,flushed
cheek,meal,membrane,morsel,
most intimate odour,palm,passage,persistent scent,pore,sauce,soft pocket,
slightest sliver,stomach,surface,thick spread,tongue,taste bud,vein,
vinaigrette'.split(',');
var trans='agitate,attract,bite,boil,braise,burn,carve,char,chew,coat,
consume,crack,cultivate,devour,digest,direct,dissect,distil,dominate,
drink,drive,engage,engorge,fill,grate,grind,incise,ink,ingest,julienne,
melt,nibble,pare,peel,pick,pluck,ripen,repel,separate,sever,singe, skim,
skin,split,stuff,stimulate,stain,stir,strain,strengthen,strike,style,
swallow,tear,texture,weaken,whip,wilt,yield'.split(',');
var imper='become,confuse,cut,decant,enter,examine,gorge on, inhabit,
inspect,note,observe,obliterate,read,release,translate,write,
savour,scrutinize,slice,sip,study';
imper=imper.split(',');
var intrans='absorb,age,assimilate,balance,blend,brew,cool, concentrate,
complement,cream,cure,dissolve,encrust,evaporate, ferment,heat,
incorporate,infuse,layer,marinate,mature,perfume, permeate,reduce,ripen,
```

```
round,steam,steep,soak,savour,sip,simmer,
stew,warm'.split(',');
var s='s,'.split(',');
var texture='acrid,barely perceptible,cautious,complex,dense,delicate,
elegant,faint,fragrant,hint of,heady,powerful,pungent,rich, sickly,
smoky,supple,velvety'.split(',');
function rand_range(max) {
 return Math.floor(Math.random()*(max+1));
}
function choose(array) {
 return array[rand_range(array.length-1)];
}
function path() {
 var p=rand_range(1);
 var words=choose(above);
 if ((words=='forest')&&(rand_range(3)==1)) {
  words='monkeys '+choose(trans);
 } else {
  words+=s[p]+' '+choose(trans)+s[(p+1)%2];
 }
 words+=' the '+choose(below)+choose(s)+'.';
 return words;
}
function site() {
 var words='';
 if (rand_range(2)==1) {
  words+=choose(above);
 } else {
  words+=choose(below);
 }
 words+='s '+choose(intrans)+'.';
 return words;
}
function cave() {
var adjs=(choose(texture)+',almond,berry,blackstrap,burnt,cassis,
cardamom,cinnamon,citrus,colourful,cordial,damson,ginger,herbaceous,
liquorice,liquor,'+'aftertaste').split(',');
var target=1+rand_range(3);
 while (adjs.length>target) {
  adjs.splice(rand_range(adjs.length),1);
  }
var words='\u00a0\u00a0'+choose(imper)+' the '+adjs.join(' ')+' -';
 return words;
}
function do_line() {
 var main=document.getElementById('main');
```

```
if (t<=25) {
 t+=1;
} else {
 main.removeChild(document.getElementById('main').firstChild);
}
if (n===0) {
 text=' ';
} else if (n==1) {
 paths=2+rand_range(2);
 text=path();
} else if (n<paths) {
 text=site();
} else if (n==paths) {
 text=path();
} else if (n==paths+1) {
 text=' ';
} else if (n==paths+2) {
 text=cave();
} else {
 text=' ';
 n=0;
}
n+=1;
text=text.substring(0,1).toUpperCase()+text.substring(1,text.length);
last=document.createElement('div');
last.appendChild(document.createTextNode(text));
main.appendChild(last);
}
function poem() {
 setInterval(do_line, 1200);
}
</script>
</head>
<body onload="poem()">
<div style="float:right; color:#306; height:60pt"><br>
GORGE<br><del><a href="http://nickm.com/poems/taroko_gorge.html">Nick
Montfort</a></del><br>
<a href="http://luckysoap.com">J.R. Carpenter</a>
<br><br>
<img src="images/intestines.gif" width=171 height=270 border=0>
<br><br>
</div>
<div id="main"></div>
</body>
</html>
```

Taroko Gorge, by Nick Montfort
http://nickm.com/poems/taroko_gorge.html

The Montfort Variables

```
var above='brow,mist,shape,layer,the crag,stone,forest,
height'.split(',');
var below='flow,basin,shape,vein,rippling,stone,cove,
rock'.split(',');
var trans='command,pace,roam,trail,frame,sweep,exercise,
range'.split(',');
var imper='track,shade,translate,stamp,progress
through,direct,run,enter';
imper=imper.split(',');
var intrans='linger,dwell,rest,relax,hold,dream,hum'.split(',');
var s='s,'.split(',');
var texture='rough,fine'.split(',');
```

Tokyo Garage, by Scott Rettberg

http://retts.net/tokyogarage.html

The Rettberg Variables

```
var above='punk rocker,public servant,prostitute,poet,war widow, addict,
movie star,tourist,teenager,zombie,goth girl,schoolboy,driver, night,
stockbroker,siren,saxaphonist,spokesmodel,rat,translator,rock star,
retiree,prostitute,dawn,protagonist,neon sign,traffic jam,bicycle
messenger,drummer,godzilla,costumed mascot,vending machine, samurai,
private dick,massively multiplayer game,chat client,devout worshiper,
shrine,buddha,jesus freak,traveler,cat,dragon,puppeteer, hallucination,
shrine,chauffeur,mute,technicolor nightmare,private security agent,
temple,student,supercomputer,ninja,cultist,scholar, speed racer,
undercover cop,earthquake,fish monger,contortionist, microchip,gamer,
yakuza,freeter,aristocrat,shogun warrior, gambler,surveillance camera,
watcher,pirate,occidental,computer scientist,monk,space invader,talk
show host,noh enthusiast, juggler,cowboy,cosplayer,blogger,hacker,
detective,alternative medicine specialist,smoker,atomic bomb,thug,
architect, technocrat'.split(',')
var below='Roppongi drunk,Shibuya shopper,gaijin,geisha,manga,pachinko
parlor,cherry blossom,sumo,kanji,nose ring,whale,supermodel,pickpocket,
flower arrangement,villian,speedwalker,designer,dancer,teacher,sailor,
banker,kabuki dancer,clown,magician,virtual pet,correspondent,dog,kung-
fu fighter,cleric,bureaucrat,freak,robot,fruitseller,author,dreamer,
panda bear,stranger,hip cat,dealer,automaton,mystic,kid,pink kitten,
monster,soldier,diplomat,nun,subway,machine,market,politician,host,
transvestite,cigarette,subject,sushi joint,ingenue,shadow,lantern,
cuisine,black widow,libation,scandal,pain,processor,routine,motorcycle
gang,vintage cadillac,mobile phone,casino,rocketeer,fund,altruist,
embezzler,spiritual seeker,DJ,
other'.split(',')
var trans='warm,warn,forgive,pick,hustle,trail,frame,sweep,smell,grope,
arrange,fondle,adore,confuse,covet,regret,endure,suffer,feel,scold,
subdue,hassle,orient,dream,hate,jam,transform,transport,reorient,
bribe,remove,chill,educate,inform,deceive,rescue,simulate,stimulate,
eroticize,follow,assault,serenade,become,enlist,corrupt,shadow,smoke,
shake,frighten,swindle,skin,critique,rearrange,preserve,freak,grok,
```

```
liquidate,fund,comfort,welcome,greet,eye,love,detest,test,unsettle,
arrest,defend,expose,profile,ceremonialize,proselytize,purchase,drain,
contaminate'.split(',')
var imper='watch,beat,translate,caress,go to,stumble through,run,enter,
defeat,promote,finger,elucidate,explain,paint,command,direct,revivify,
sing,sing damn you sing,script,remember,disregard,concantenate,suffer,
recall,absorb,forgive,scramble,rattle,harmonize,synthesize,pardon,
excuse,explore,digest,apologize for,process,consider,embellish,forget,
signify,deconstruct,protect,endure,sculpt,eliminate,forego,imagine,
curse,bless,waste'
imper=imper.split(',')
var intrans='fall,dwell,rock,circle,clamor,dream,sing,imitate,debate,
evacuate,harass,twist,reverse,pay,expire,sing,recover,destroy,
investigate,fail,succeed,win,drop,burn,explode,rest,regenerate,halt,
perspire,conspire,walk'.split(',')
var s='s,'.split(',')
var texture='smooth,waxy,rough,slick,silken,gummy,squishy,scaly,bumpy,
wet'.split(',')
```

J.R. Carpenter has taken apart and reassembled my poetry generator *Taroko Gorge.* (The first to appropriate and rework that piece, as far as I know, was Scott Rettberg, who created *Tokyo Garage.*) J.R.'s piece – one might call it a *tract* of sorts – is simply called *Gorge.* See if you can stomach it, and for how long.

Also, check out J.R.'s project *Story Generation(s),* which involved reworking two of my 1k Python programs and which launched May 8 at PW10 Performance Writing Weekend. The project includes a JavaScript port of "Excerpts from the Chronicles of Pookie & JR." This is generally not a bad idea; I wrote *Taroko Gorge* originally in Python (a programming language I prefer for when I'm thinking) and converted it to JavaScript for easy web viewing.

Nick Montfort, "Once More into the Gorge," Post Position
http://nickm.com/post/2010/05/once-more-into-the-gorge/

Degeneration (with Medlar Lucan and Durian Gray)

SIC FARCIES EAM SEPIAM COCTAM
(SQUID STUFFED WITH BRAINS)

Gorge incises the membrane.
Heads ripen the crusts.

Remove the membranes from a calf's brains,
fry them and mash with pepper.

Brains stuff the passages.
Languages repel the guts.

Mix with raw eggs, peppercorns, and minced meat.

Noses chew the gut.
Desires heat.
Slightest slivers dissolve.
Sight incises the proffered fingers.

Then stuff the mixture into the squid,
stitch up and cook in boiling water until the stuffing is firm.

Sweat picks the flushed cheeks.
Nose stirs the membrane.

Still hungry?

Enzyme distils the palm.
Sights mature.
Gullets singe the crusts.

LUMBULI
(SMALL ROAST TESTICLES)

Sights pare the membranes.
Crusts assimilate.
Enzymes mature.
Digestive juice weakens the veins.

Slice each testicle in two and sprinkle with pepper,
nuts,
finely chopped coriander and powdered fennel seed.

Gullet inks the dip.
Veins ripen.
Gazes assimilate.
Passions consume the aromas.

Sew the halves together, wrap each one in a caul
(i.e. the external membrane of a stomach)
and fry them in olive oil and fish-pickle until brown.

Passions ink the membranes.
Incisors tear the persistent scents.

Then grill or roast in the oven.

Sights split the dressing.
Surfaces marinate.
Digestive juices ingest the membranes.

scrutinize the delicate -

Muscle melts the crust.
Gorges pare the palms.

Medlar Lucan & Durian Gray, Alex martin & Jerome Fletcher, eds., *The Decadent Cookbook,* Cambridge: Dedalus, 1995, page 20.

J.R. Carpenter Um, wait, is it really wise to travel with these guys? http://bit.ly/1f6bC

10 September 2009 at 20:57 · Comment · Like

J.R. Carpenter Off to Budapest with Decadent Travelers Medlar Lucan & Durian Gray to swan about at the Four Seasons http://preview.tinyurl.com/qukbdj

10 September 2009 at 20:51 · Comment · Like

J.R. Carpenter Off to Budapest with Decadent Travelers Medlar Lucan & Durian Gray to crash - I mean do a performance at - a private dinner / birthday party at the Four Seasons: http://www.fourseasons.com/budapest/

Four Seasons Hotel Gresham Palace Budapest: A Luxury Hotel in Budapest, Hungary

www.fourseasons.com

(Budapest, Hungary) Four Seasons is the world's leading operator of luxury hotels and resorts. Visit our site to plan your vacation, getaway, or business travel to Gresham Palace in Budapest, Hungary.

10 September 2009 at 20:51 · Comment · Like · Share

Annie Briard likes this.

Write a comment...

IN CONCLUSION

Two Generations Ago

Two Generations Ago

The Williamsburg sidewalk glitters at night. A trivia of mineral terminology tumbles in Lynne's head. Mica, silica – *there's a name for this,* she thinks as she walks toward an evening with a woman she's never met, but with whom she knows she has been compared.

The woman is waiting for Lynne in a tavern in Greenpoint. From the sidewalk, Lynne sees her: back to the window, sitting at the bar. The woman is small, and greenly lit. Lynne is not early, but the woman clearly doesn't expect her yet. Back bent, slumped – she's let her posture's run amuck.

Gabe had insisted Lynne call her. "I won't have time," Lynne had said.

"You'll be staying in her neighbourhood. One quick drink."

"I filed a complaint against him, you know," the woman tells Lynne two drinks in. She's sitting up straight now. They're at a different bar. Better lit.

"He was practically stalking me," the woman says. Lynne could see it all, she *had* seen it herself: his small presents, sophisticated and ingratiating; his extravagantly oblique gestures, all ego drenched in expectations.

The woman's name is Maria. She and Lynne look almost exactly alike.

"She's great. You'll love her," Gabe had told Lynne, because he had, she had assumed. But now she saw. He hadn't been in love with her. He'd been in unrequited enthral.

Lynne and Maria walk down through North Side together. Same height, same skin-tone, same freckles, same black-frame glasses, same haircut, same short black hair invisible in the same darkness as they pass beneath the BQE. Emerging into a low wasteland of post-industrial buildings, their same-size shadows pass impassive flat black walls.

"Isn't it dangerous, to walk though here?"

"But I have you to protect me," Maria puts her arm though Lynne's. Her huge watch hangs loose on her lean wrist. Its dial glows brighter than the lamplight.

In the empty sound of their footsteps Lynne's tell Maria: "He told me, how the sidewalks sparkle here." Glacial out-wash – granite? Quartz? Ahead, the river. Across, Manhattan looms. Between, the Williamsburg Bridge keeps the Lower East Side on a tight leash.

"It's broken glass," Maria says. "The sidewalks are recycled."

"My grandmother lived around here," Lynne adds, a block later. She has no idea where they are. And her grandmother never lived in Brooklyn. But lots of her grandmother's relatives once did.

"Oh yeah?" Maria gives her arm a squeeze. A whole story pops out.

"Every Shabbas, Saturday afternoon, my Grandmother, her sister Ruthy and a couple hundred other Jews walked across the Williamsburg Bridge. Religiously, to visit family." Lynne gives this newly minted life story a forty to sixty percent chance of being at least twenty percent true.

They round a corner onto a busy street. The neighbourhood presents another face.

"Where are we?"

"The hippest art-welder bar in Brooklyn," Maria develops a swagger as she drags Lynne inside. Everyone looks vaguely familiar. If Lynne lived in Brooklyn, she'd know every other person. But she hasn't hypothetically lived in Brooklyn for two generations. Maria tells everyone in the bar that Lynne's her sister, winking so wildly each time she does this that no one can tell if she means that this isn't true at all or that it's really, really, really true and boy is it a long story.

Suddenly, Lynne is very tired. All that walking.

If Gabe pursued Lynne because she reminded him of Maria, who had Maria reminded Gabe of, Lynne wonders? Maria takes her hand. Their palms fit together – exactly the same size.

The Former Resident Project, Rachelle Viader Knowles
CONFLUX 2006 – Brooklyn, New York, USA
http://confluxfestival.org/projects.php?projectid=101

The FORMER RESIDENT project explores the city through the narratives of the no-longer resident, people whose lives have been shaped by their experiences of places they no longer inhabit. For many of us, 'residence' is a multiple thing, a series of narratives and residues that shift and slip over time. When we leave a place, what do we take?… And what do we leave behind? The project includes multiple participants, all former 'residents' of Brooklyn. Each participant has donated a story about something that happened in a particular location, the stories they choose to tell from the memories that stuck…

The FORMER RESIDENT project happens both on-line [http://www.former-resident-project.net] and on the street. Do YOU find yourself in Brooklyn? Each story has been printed onto a fridge magnet and posted at the address listed on the website… waiting to find a new home and to become a part of someone else's life. Maybe yours?

t h e - f o r m e r - r e s i d e n t - p r o j e c t

Brooklyn NY USA

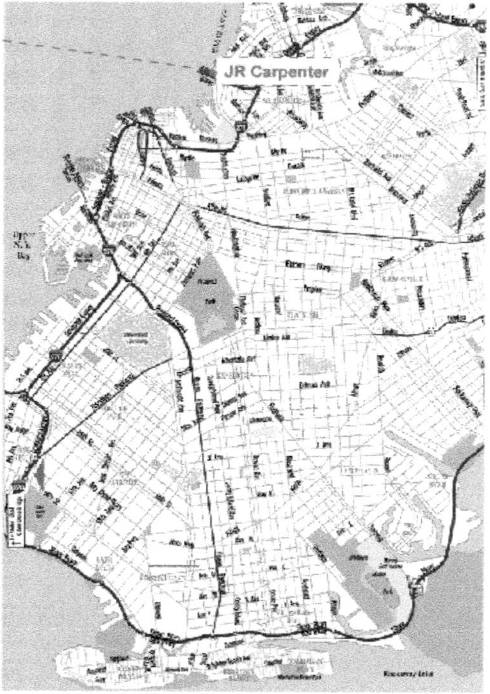

JR Carpenter

3rd St & 7th Ave
Williamsburg Bridge
Parkside Subway
15 S. Portland Ave
Sheepshead Bay Road & Gravesend Neck Road
6th St & 6th Ave
964 Eastern Parkway
A Sheepshead Bay Pier
20 Henry St
3rd St & 6th Ave
Clark St
Clark St
Brooklyn Heights Promenade
Borough Park
334 87 St
334 87 St
334 87 St
334 87 St
Metropolitan Swimming Pool
Shore Road & 87 St
Floyd Bennett Field

Brooklyn Academy of Music
330 87th St
330 87th St
330 87th St
330 87th St
330 87th St
330 87th St
334 87th St
Verazzano Bridge
330 87th St
330 87th St
N. 7th St & Driggs Ave
Cobble Hill NYSC
Brooklyn Bridge
917 Metropolitan Ave
Bedford Ave & N. 8th St
Grand Army Plaza
Remsen St & Hicks St
Brooklyn Bridge
Berry St & N. 3rd St
Roebling St & N. 5th St

The Williamsburg sidewalk glitters in the night: mica, silica – *there's a name for this.*
I walk through geological vocabulary, a trivia of mineral terminology tumbles in my head.
She's waiting in a tavern in Greenpoint. Small, and greenly lit, she sits at the bar.
Back to the window, back bent, slumped. She's doesn't expect me yet; her posture's run amuck. Gabe insisted I call her. He hadn't been in love with her. In lust. In unrequited enthral. We walk down through North Side. Our same-cut short black hair invisible in the nervous late night passage beneath the overpass of the BQE.

"I won't have time," I said.

"You're staying in her neighbourhood. One quick drink."

"I filed a complaint you know," she's sitting up straight now, at a different bar. Better lit. "He was practically stalking me," she says, and I notice that we look a lot alike.

I could see it all: small presents, sophisticated ingratiating, extravagantly oblique gestures, ego drenched in expectations.

"She's great. You'll love her."

Emerging into a low wasteland of post-industrial buildings, our same-size shadows pass impassive flat black walls.

"Isn't it dangerous, to walk though here?"

"But I have you to protect me," she puts her arm though mine.

Her watch hangs loose on her lean wrist, which rests on my crooked sleeve – the low glow of the dial brighter than the lamplight. In the empty sound of our footsteps I tell her:

"He told me, how the sidewalks sparkle here."

Glacial out-wash – granite? Quartz?
Manhattan looms. The Williamsburg Bridge keeps the Lower East Side on a tight leash.

"My grandmother lived around here," I say.

"Oh yeah?" She gives my arm a squeeze. A whole story pops out.

"Every Shabbas. Saturday afternoon. My Grandmother, her sister Ruthy and a couple hundred other Jews walked across the Williamsburg Bridge. Religiously, to visit family."

We round a corner onto a busy street. The neighborhood presents another face.

"Where are we?"

"The hippest art-welder bar in Brooklyn."
Inside, everyone looks vaguely familiar. If I lived here I'd know every other person.
But I haven't lived here for two generations.
She winks wildly, tells everyone that she's my sister.
Suddenly I'm very tired. All that walking.
She takes my hand. Our palms fit together – hers the same size as mine.

FORMER RESIDENT J. R. Carpenter lived in Brooklyn two generations ago. **Now lives in Montreal.**

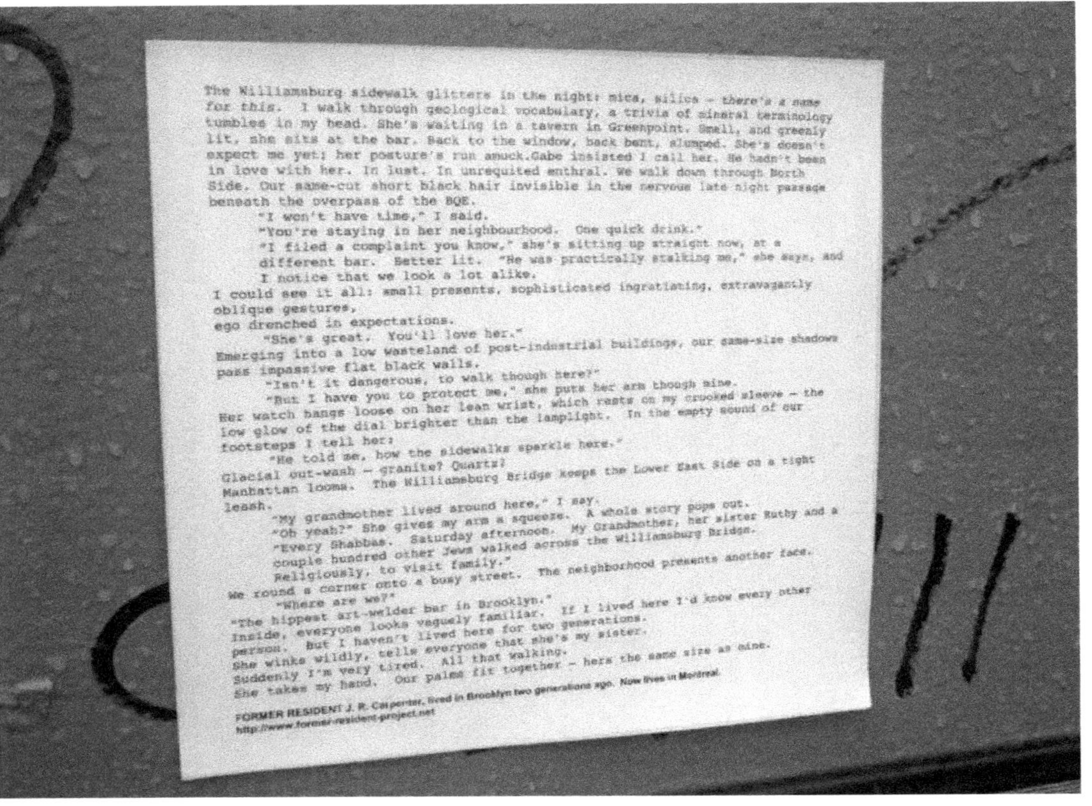

The Williamsburg sidewalk glitters in the night: mica, silica – *there's a name for this*. I walk through geological vocabulary, a trivia of mineral terminology tumbles in my head. She's waiting in a tavern in Greenpoint. Small, and greenly lit, she sits at the bar. Back to the window, back bent, slumped. She's doesn't expect me yet; her posture's run amuck.Gabe insisted I call her. He hadn't been in love with her. In lust. In unrequited enthral. We walk down through North Side. Our same-cut short black hair invisible in the nervous late night passage beneath the overpass of the BQE.

"I won't have time," I said.

"You're staying in her neighbourhood. One quick drink."

"I filed a complaint you know," she's sitting up straight now, at a different bar. Better lit. "He was practically stalking me," she says, and I notice that we look a lot alike.

I could see it all: small presents, sophisticated ingratiating, extravagantly oblique gestures,
ego drenched in expectations.

"She's great. You'll love her."

Emerging into a low wasteland of post-industrial buildings, our same-size shadows pass impassive flat black walls.

"Isn't it dangerous, to walk though here?"

"But I have you to protect me," she puts her arm though mine.

Her watch hangs loose on her lean wrist, which rests on my crooked sleeve – the low glow of the dial brighter than the lamplight. In the empty sound of our footsteps I tell her:

"He told me, how the sidewalks sparkle here."

Glacial out-wash – granite? Quartz?

Manhattan looms. The Williamsburg Bridge keeps the Lower East Side on a tight leash.

"My grandmother lived around here," I say.

"Oh yeah?" She gives my arm a squeeze. A whole story pops out.

"Every Shabbas. Saturday afternoon. My Grandmother, her sister Ruthy and a couple hundred other Jews walked across the Williamsburg Bridge.

Religiously, to visit family."

We round a corner onto a busy street. The neighborhood presents another face.

"Where are we?"

"The hippest art-welder bar in Brooklyn."

Inside, everyone looks vaguely familiar. If I lived here I'd know every other person. But I haven't lived here for two generations.

She winks wildly, tells everyone that she's my sister.

Suddenly I'm very tired. All that walking.

She takes my hand. Our palms fit together – hers the same size as mine.

FORMER RESIDENT J. R. Carpenter, lived in Brooklyn two generations ago. Now lives in Montreal.
http://www.former-resident-project.net

ACKNOWLEDGEMENTS

GENERATION(S) is the book equivalent of a Nick Montfort tribute band. Thank you Nick, for your caring coding sharing friendship.

The source code for *Excerpts from the Chronicles of Pookie and JR* and *I've Died and Gone to Devon* are based on story1.py, and the source code for *Auto-Autobiography* is based on story2.py, 1k Python story generators by Nick Montfort: http://grandtextauto.org/2008/11/30/three-1k-story-generators/

Excerpts from the Chronicles of Pookie and JR started out as a diary written in chalk on a wall in Ingrid Bachmann's loft in Montreal. Thank you Ingrid, for that first post-everything refuge.

Pookie is a hermit crab. Pookie's full name is Pookie 14.

Ingrid Bachmann: Digital Crustaceans v.0.2: Homesteading on the Web first appeared in *FUSE*, Vol. 27, No. 1, Toronto, ON, Canada, March 2004.

Most of the sentences in *I've Died and Gone to Devon* started out as Tweets posted to @jr_carpenter and @theriverdart and pulled into Facebook. Thank you, all you real friend Facebook friends, for your wisecracks and witty rejoinders.

Some phrases in *I've Died and Gone to Devon* are borrowed from The Darting Story Cartographers: http://dartingmap.blogspot.com/

Auto-Autobiography was inspired by a paragraph from Anne-Marie MacDonald, *As The Crow Flies*, Toronto: Knopf, 2003, page 36.

The source code for *Gorge* is based on *Taroko Gorge* by Nick Montfort: http://nickm.com/poems/taroko_gorge.html

The Rettberg Variables are excerpted from the source code of *Tokyo Garage,* Scott Rettberg's remix of *Taroko Gorge* by Nick Montfort: http://retts.net/tokyogarage.html

Degeneration (with Medlar Lucan & Durian Gray) cites recipes excerpted from: Medlar Lucan & Durian Gray, Alex martin & Jerome Fletcher, eds., *The Decadent Cookbook,* Cambridge: Dedalus, 1995, p 20.

A live degeneration of *Gorge* was performed by J. R. Carpenter and Durian Gray at Machfeld | Studio, Max Winter Platz 21/1, 1020 Wien, June 26, 2010.

Two Generations Ago first appeared in *The Former Resident Project,* by Rachelle Viader Knowles: http://www.former-resident-project.net, which was presented at CONFLUX 2006 – Brooklyn, New York. http://confluxfestival.org/projects.php?projectid=101

Special thanks to:

Ingrid Bachmann
Jerome Fletcher
Durian Gray
MACHFELD
Nick Montfort
Jörg Piringer
Pookie 14
Ravi Rajakumar
Scott Rettberg
Rachelle Viader Knowles
TRAUMAWIEN.

BIO

J.R. Carpenter JR Carpenter is a poet, essayist, fiction writer and web artist. Using
the internet as a medium, her work is informed by notions of place. Maps and mapping feature strongly in her web based projects operating, often simultaneously as images, interfaces and metaphors for distant places and surrogate histories. A showcase of...
See more

Arnolfini | Performance Writing: JR Carpenter
www.arnolfini.org.uk
Arnolfini

04 December 2009 at 12:28 · Comment · Like · Share

Emilie O'Brien, Caitlin Hartnett, Thomas J. Lefebvre and 3 others like this.

Jeremy Hight i concur
04 December 2009 at 20:25 · Delete

Jeremy Hight j.r is all of those things..yes...bio...you are on target
04 December 2009 at 20:25 · Delete

J.R. Carpenter ha! hardly anyone talks to bios any more. cute. thanks all, xx, JR
04 December 2009 at 21:07 · Delete

Linda Dornan great! good for you girl!
04 December 2009 at 22:38 · Delete

Write a comment...

www.ingramcontent.com/pod-product-compliance
Ingram Content Group UK Ltd.
Pitfield, Milton Keynes, MK11 3LW, UK
UKHW021653190726
13853UKWH00001B/228